Wait a minute—was she seriously considering Tyler's proposal?

Well, why not? Even if Walter wasn't convicted, her future was uncertain. Not only that, she was terrified at the prospect of living alone. Tyler was a cop—he could provide her with the protection she desperately craved.

Keep your friends close, and your enemies closer popped into her head. She dismissed it immediately. Tyler wasn't her enemy. He wanted to marry her, didn't he?

She wouldn't kid herself into thinking his proposal had to do with anything other than the baby. But if she accepted his proposal—and that was a big *if*—it didn't mean she'd cross over to his side of the investigation. Of course, anything she might just happen to learn as his fiancée would be an added bonus.

A disturbing thought occurred to her. He could very well be thinking the same thing about her.

Dear Reader,

Well, the wait is over—*New York Times* bestselling author Diana Palmer is back, and Special Edition has got her! In *Carrera's Bride*, another in Ms. Palmer's enormously popular LONG, TALL TEXANS miniseries, an innocent Jacobsville girl on a tropical getaway finds herself in need of protection—and gets it from an infamous casino owner who is not all that he appears! I think you'll find this one was well worth the wait....

We're drawing near the end of our in-series continuity THE PARKS EMPIRE. This month's entry is *The Marriage Act* by Elissa Ambrose, in which a shy secretary learns that her one night of sleeping with the enemy has led to unexpected consequences. Next up is *The Sheik & the Princess Bride* by Susan Mallery, in which a woman hired to teach a prince how to fly finds herself *his* student, as well, as he gives her lessons...in love! In *A Baby on the Ranch*, part of Stella Bagwell's popular MEN OF THE WEST miniseries, a single mother-to-be finds her long-lost family—and, just possibly, the love of her life. And a single man in the market for household help finds himself about to take on the role of husband—and father of four—in Penny Richards's *Wanted: One Father*. Oh, and speaking of single parents—a lonely widow with a troubled adolescent son finds the solution to both her problems in her late husband's law-enforcement partner, in *The Way to a Woman's Heart* by Carol Voss.

So enjoy, and come back next month for six wonderful selections from Silhouette Special Edition.

Happy Thanksgiving!

Gail Chasan
Senior Editor

Please address questions and book requests to:
Silhouette Reader Service
U.S.: 3010 Walden Ave., P.O. Box 1325, Buffalo, NY 14269
Canadian: P.O. Box 609, Fort Erie, Ont. L2A 5X3

The Marriage Act

ELISSA AMBROSE

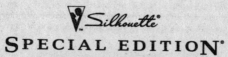

Silhouette

SPECIAL EDITION

Published by Silhouette Books

America's Publisher of Contemporary Romance

Special thanks and acknowledgment are given to
Elissa Ambrose for her contribution to
THE PARKS EMPIRE series.

 SILHOUETTE BOOKS

ISBN 0-373-24646-3

THE MARRIAGE ACT

Visit Silhouette Books at www.eHarlequin.com

Printed in U.S.A.

Books by Elissa Ambrose

Silhouette Special Edition

Journey of the Heart #1506
A Mother's Reflection #1578
The Best of Both Worlds #1607
The Marriage Act #1646

ELISSA AMBROSE

Originally from Montreal, Canada, Elissa Ambrose now resides in Arizona with her husband, her smart but surly cat and her sweet but silly cockatoo. She's the proud mother of two daughters, who, though they have flown the coop, still manage to keep her on her toes. She started out as a computer programmer and now serves as the fiction editor at *Anthology* magazine, a literary journal published in Mesa, Arizona. When she's not writing or editing or just hanging out with her husband, she can be found at the indoor ice arena, trying out a new spin or jump.

THE PARKS EMPIRE

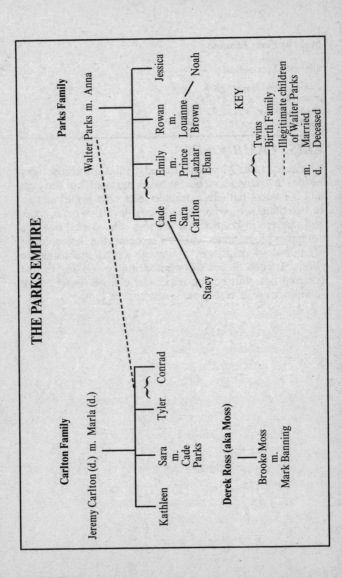

Parks Family

Walter Parks m. Anna

Cade
m.
Sara
Carlton

Stacy

Emily
m.
Prince
Lazhar
Eban

Rowan
m.
Louanne
Brown

Jessica

Noah

Carlton Family

Jeremy Carlton (d.) m. Marla (d.)

Kathleen

Sara
m.
Cade Parks

Tyler   Conrad

Derek Ross (aka Moss)

Brooke Moss
m.
Mark Banning

KEY

{ Twins
— Birth Family
----- Illegitimate children of Walter Parks
m. Married
d. Deceased

Prologue

He removed the heavy gold chain from around his neck. "I want to give you something. You might say it's the closest thing to my heart. I know it sounds crazy, but I feel as if I've known you forever."

He fastened the chain around her neck, and the medallion fell between her breasts. "Beautiful," he whispered, but then his face clouded over.

"What is it?" she asked, tracing the line of his jaw with her fingers.

"There's something I have to tell you. I'm not who you think I am."

"Shh," she said, replacing her fingers with her lips. "We're exactly who we need to be."

Chapter One

Linda Mailer was late.

She hurried up the walkway that led to the upscale seafood restaurant, the smell of broiled fish and grilled shrimp mingling with the salty sea air. Waves slapped against the pier below, while behind her the sun slowly descended into the cliffs beyond the Bay.

She glanced at her watch, wondering why she had bothered to show up at all. She didn't belong here. She wasn't sure she belonged anywhere. At first, she had refused Sara and Cade's invitation, but when Cade's sister Emily had insisted she come, she'd caved in.

How could she say no to a princess? Albeit, Emily was a princess by marriage, but she was a princess nonetheless.

Emily Parks—correction, Emily Eban, Princess of Daniz—had told her she was practically family. Nonsense! The only person Linda was close to in that family was Walter, her employer and Emily's father, and he wouldn't even be here tonight. Besides, if she were practically family, wouldn't that make her practically a princess? Her mouth curved down in self-deprecation. A princess was the last thing she felt like.

In the lobby of the trendy seafood restaurant, Linda tried to ignore her queasiness and checked her coat with the attendant. She looked down at her dress, a shapeless frock that hung loosely on her frame and fell to her ankles. When she'd first seen it on the clearance rack in the department store, she'd known it would be perfect. A dark gray-green, it would allow her to blend into the background.

Gazing around at the decor, she headed toward the Poseidon Patio, where the party was being held. Ornately patterned with shells and conches, the walls had been painted to reflect the depths of the sea. She more than blended in. She could virtually disappear into the backdrop.

She had something to hide, and the dress she was wearing would do the job.

Not that she was showing yet. But she knew she couldn't take any chances. At the office, she sat all day immersed in ledgers, hardly ever raising her head, but here she would be on display. People would be looking.

And if they looked closely, they might guess her little secret.

Her little secret, as she preferred to call it, was the reason she was late getting to the party. Morning sickness—now that was an interesting euphemism. Sure, she was queasy in the morning, but the feeling persisted all day and night, not even subsiding when she was asleep. Last night, she'd dreamed she was on a cruise in the midst of a storm. The ship was rocking and she was reeling.

Mercy, not here, she thought now, as nausea overcame her. Queasiness was one thing; this was something else. It was as if the restaurant's decor had sprung to life, as large ocean waves seemed to roll off the walls, threatening to swallow her up.

That decided it. She wouldn't stay. She had no intention of spending her Saturday evening either trying to avoid small talk with people she hardly knew or hiding in the bathroom, bending over the porcelain throne. After the nausea had somewhat subsided, she headed back to the coat check.

"Linda, hurry! We're just about to start dinner."

Linda cast a rueful glance at Sara Carlton, Emily's sister-in-law. Correction, Sara Parks, now that she was married to Cade. Lately, it seemed as if everyone Linda knew was getting married, and although she was happy for them, sometimes she couldn't help but feel annoyed. It had nothing to do with her not-married-and-never-had-been status; on the contrary, matrimony was not one of her life's priorities. Simply, newly married couples always seemed to probe into what they considered her sad-single state, and now that Sara had spotted her, it was too late for a getaway.

Smiling brightly, Sara approached her. Chic in a three-quarter-length silk dress, she didn't merely walk; she floated, as though some of her sister-in-law's new royal status had flowed into her through osmosis.

"Come, I'll show you to your table," she said, "but first, I want you to meet my twin brothers."

Actually, half brothers. The office had been buzzing for weeks about Tyler and Conrad Carlton, the "surprise" sons of Walter Parks. The identical twins and Sara had shared the same mother, but what made the situation even more complex was that Cade Parks, Sara's husband, was also a half brother to the twins, through Walter.

Illegitimate, Linda said to herself, recalling the gossip. Such an outdated term, yet apparently it was still used. She shuddered. It was such an ugly word. Would people use it to describe *her* child?

Her thoughts returned to Walter and his family. Even though the DNA testing had confirmed his paternity, he refused to acknowledge his two grown sons. Linda felt a wave of guilt. Like Walter, she should have refused to come to the party, which was being given by Sara and Cade to welcome the twins into the family. Shouldn't her loyalty lie with Walter? Although, she had to admit, Cade and Emily—his *legitimate* children—always treated her well, making sure to include her in every family function. As much as she hated social gatherings, it would have been rude of her to refuse this invitation, just as she had never been able to refuse any of the others.

Strangely, even Walter had insisted that she go. It was as if he wanted to attend the party but was sending her in his place. The notion, of course, was preposterous. He wanted nothing to do with that side of his family. He'd made that clear—to her, to his family, even to the press.

Sara led the way to the ornate banquet room, toward

her handsome new husband. When Linda's gaze turned to the man next to Cade, her heart stopped beating.

Standing next to Cade was Thomas McMann.

The man she'd run from two months ago.

Sara's face was beaming. "Linda, I'd like you to meet my brother, Conrad Carlton. Conrad, this is Linda Mailer, the woman I've been telling you about. I've placed you at the same table, since you two have so much in common."

This couldn't be. There had to be an explanation. A lot of men looked alike. When they'd met two months ago, she hadn't been wearing her glasses, and the bar had been dim. *They're all the same when the lights go out,* her mother used to say.

She studied him surreptitiously. He looked like a lot like Thomas, but something was different. Something she couldn't name. The longer she studied him, the more obvious it became that he wasn't the man she'd spent the night with.

She collected her breath, then looked back at Sara. Like every other newlywed Linda had ever known, Sara wanted to play matchmaker. But even if Linda were interested in meeting someone, which she emphatically was not, Conrad was the last man she'd choose. So much in common, Sara had said. Not in this lifetime, Linda thought. According to the gossip in the office, Conrad was wild and carefree, always up for a party. She, on the other hand, was as exciting as a potato. Her idea of a challenge was balancing a checkbook.

No, Conrad Carlton, alias Party Animal, alias Ladies' Man, wasn't her type.

Then again, she wasn't sure she had a type.

Say something, she ordered herself. Make small talk. Smoothing a wrinkle in the fabric of her dress, she mumbled, "Uh, I hear you're a rancher."

He looked at her through cold, green eyes, as though she had materialized from nowhere. "And I hear you're an accountant. I'm sure you get this all the time, but I have to ask. Why would someone with your looks choose such a staid profession?"

She regarded him warily. Someone with her looks? Was he nuts? Was he *flirting?*

"I like figures," she said, then looked down at the floor. Good grief, how could she have said something so moronic?

Apparently he was deaf, because he looked at her as though she'd uttered the most interesting tidbit he'd heard in years. "So, done any personal audits lately?" he asked.

Sara and Cade stood by quietly, watching the exchange. From the expression on their faces, Linda could tell they were pleased. She'd hoped that now that she was thirty, the pressure from others to follow in their matrimonial footsteps would slack off, but so far it hadn't. Why did newly married couples always feel the need to spread their happiness? She was referring to those well-meaning yet nosy people who for some altruistic reason—or sadistic, depending on what view you took—were eager for her to experience the same bliss they claimed to be experiencing. So what if half those blissful couples ended up in divorce court?

She looked back up at Conrad's face. The way his eyes were assessing her body seemed to suggest that he wouldn't mind doing a personal audit of *her.*

She flinched under his gaze. It was unnerving how much he looked like Thomas. Something else unnerved her, as well. Conrad had a twin brother...an identical twin brother...

No. I hadn't been wearing my glasses that night, she reminded herself, and then cast her unsettling thought aside.

She was sure that Sara had asked him to be attentive. Why else would he be flirting with her? Her cheeks grew warm. Just what she needed—a pity date. He was obviously waiting for her to reply, but she felt as tongue-tied as a competitor in a peanut-butter-eating contest. If she couldn't get through one minute of small talk, she didn't have a chance of making it through dinner.

He wasn't flirting, she decided. He was mocking her. It wouldn't be the first time someone had made her profession the target of a joke. Not that she cared. Maybe to some people accounting seemed boring, but the truth was, if she had to confess to one passion in life, it would be numbers. She loved the feeling she got when preparing a spreadsheet, or when all her bank statements reconciled, or when she was off by a mere cent and, after methodical and careful backtracking, could pinpoint the error. There was truth in numbers. Working with them gave her a sense of order.

Her gaze shot to the doorway. Maybe after everyone was seated, she could make her escape. Maybe no one would notice.

"Excuse me," he said abruptly. "I think my date has arrived." He turned away, and a moment later he was talking to a sultry blonde in a short black cocktail dress that seemed to have more material in back than it did in front.

Sara's mouth dropped open in shock, and her cheeks went pink with embarrassment. "I'm sorry, Linda. I had no idea he'd invited someone to the party. I was sure the two of you would hit it off. You're a very basic sort of person, and so is he. Like I said, the two of you have a lot in common." When Linda didn't respond, Sara continued, "No, really. How much more basic does it get than living off the land? Underneath all that bravado, he's really a down-to-earth, practical person. Like you. Oh, I know he has a bit of an attitude, but that's just a veneer. He's having a hard time accepting everything that's happened."

Linda frowned. Conrad might have issues, but the notion that he had anything in common with her was preposterous. Furthermore, going through a rough patch didn't give a person a license to be rude.

But maybe he couldn't help himself. Maybe he didn't even know he was being rude. She seemed to have that effect on men.

She realized it had a lot to do with the way she dressed, the way she carried herself. She'd learned that people paid a price for enjoying themselves, and now she went out of her way to show the world—specifically the male portion—that she wasn't interested.

"It can't be easy for him," she said charitably. "Or his brother," she added, thinking about what Sara had told her about Tyler Carlton. Moody, she'd described him. Linda couldn't decide which trait was less desirable, moodiness or rudeness. Evidently, each brother wore his scars differently.

"Speaking of brothers," Sara said, waving at someone across the noisy room, "do you realize how remarkable this whole thing is? Not only are the twins my brothers, they're also my brothers-in-law! Complicated, isn't it?"

A man across the room waved back. "Uh, yes, complicated," Linda agreed, peering through her glasses to get a better look at him. Weaving his way through the crowd, he slowly approached them, and for the second time that evening her heart came to a halt.

Was this déjà vu or had she simply lost her mind? How could she make the same mistake twice in one evening?

But this time she wasn't mistaken. This time it was him.

Thomas McMann. The man she'd slept with on the night of her thirtieth birthday.

The memory of that warm August night came back in a rush. How her best friend and roommate, Sadie Heath, had convinced her to have a makeover for her birthday. How they'd gone to the piano lounge in that fashionable hotel on Nob Hill. How Linda had met a man at a table by the bar.

How his lips had felt against her neck as the elevator made its slow ascent to the third floor, where he'd rented a room.

She remembered how she'd felt the next morning when she'd spotted the gun on the bureau.

Sheer, cold terror.

Suddenly, the events of the past few weeks fell into place. The thugs coming in and out of Walter's office. The strange document she'd found in his home. The stories circulating about his embezzling.

Walter had enemies.

Thomas must have known who she was right from the start, before they'd even met at that bar. He'd been tailing her to get to Walter. Had even gone as far as seducing her. All part of a day's work.

On one level she knew that what she was thinking didn't make sense. Walter wasn't even here. But when it came to guns, all logic evaded her. Terror pervaded her body, just as it had that morning two months ago when she'd fled from the hotel.

She had to warn them. Had to warn them all, but the words wouldn't come. Why did she always get so tongue-tied? She prayed for the scream to erupt, but her whole body felt paralyzed.

He was getting closer. Five feet…four feet…

Panic rose in her throat.

He undid the button to his jacket, reached inside…

And that was all she remembered, before blacking out.

He'd thought she looked familiar, and now, seeing her up close, he knew why. The woman lying on the blue tufted carpet was Lyla.

For the past two months he'd combed the entire city, looking for her without success. In his relatively short career as a law officer, he'd put countless felons behind bars, but he hadn't been able to locate the one person he'd been desperately seeking.

He didn't like to ask himself why he'd been so desperate to find her. It wasn't as if she'd gotten under his skin. No, nothing like that. He just wasn't used to women running out on him, and he deserved an explanation.

At least, that was what he'd told himself.

Lyla. Hoping to run into her, he'd become a regular at the lounge in that swanky hotel on Nob Hill. He'd figured a girl like her needed action, that sooner or later she'd return to the scene of the crime, so to speak. Return in search of a bigger pot of gold.

Lyla. A looker like her would have no trouble reeling in dates. She could have any man she wanted, and so he'd figured she'd show up at the lounge. She could probably smell the money, from the bottom of the Hill. Which was probably why she'd pulled a disappearing act in the morning. She'd figured out that he was no Donald Trump.

Lyla. Since that night he'd searched every bar in every hotel, asking endless questions—just so he could find her and tell her a thing or two. So he'd tried to convince himself.

"Someone call an ambulance!"

Sara's voice jolted him out of his shock, and his instincts took over. He leaned over and felt for a pulse. Then, after satisfying himself that she hadn't been injured in the fall, he scooped her up in his arms. "She'll be all right," he said to the small crowd that had gathered. "Please move aside. Give her some air. Where can I take her that's quiet?" he asked Sara. He tried to sound detached and professional, but he knew he was failing miserably.

Which irritated him. He had no feelings for this woman. None whatsoever.

"There's a lounge in the ladies' room," Sara answered, looking at him quizzically.

He hurried out of the banquet room, Lyla nestled in his arms, Sara following closely behind. He kicked open the door to the ladies' room. An elderly woman in an old-fashioned beehive hairdo took one look at him and screeched.

"'Scuse me, ma'am," he said, pushing past her. Clutching her purse, the woman sprinted down the hallway.

A teenage girl entered the lounge, stopping in her tracks when she saw Tyler. "Oops, sorry, I guess I have the wrong—" Her gaze fell on Lyla. "Uh, I'll come back later," she said, backing out the door.

Under the curious gawk of two other women, he gently deposited Lyla onto the couch. "Must be those house martinis," the taller woman said. "Can we do anything?"

"Everyone, out!" he barked, then immediately regretted his tone. The stranger was only trying to be helpful. She was probably right. Lyla wasn't sick; she was just drunk.

Nevertheless, he was still concerned. Which puzzled him. What did he care? She was nothing to him.

Agitated, he ran his fingers through his hair. Maybe he'd been mistaken. Maybe the woman on the couch wasn't the same mysterious creature he'd made love to only weeks before. The woman he'd met in August had been exciting and lusty, with wild red curls tumbling down her neck. This woman's hair was tied straight back in a ponytail, her dark inviting eyes—her dark now-closed eyes—hiding behind thick-framed glasses. And that thing she was wearing looked more like a sack than a dress, the way it concealed her body from her chin to her ankles.

The night he'd met her she'd been wearing a tight

leather miniskirt and a skimpy halter top. He'd seen right from the get-go that she was dressed to advertise. The woman he'd met would never be caught in a tent like this.

Or would she? He had to admit he didn't really know her. Except, of course, in the biblical sense.

At the sink, Sara began soaking a handful of paper towels. "You'd better wait outside," she said over her shoulder. "I'll take care of Linda."

"Who?" Didn't she mean Lyla?

"Linda Mailer. Walter's accountant."

He felt as if he'd been punched in the stomach. *My father's* accountant, he said to himself. Not that he or anyone else needed to be reminded that Walter Parks was his father. News of the paternity had been splattered across every newspaper in the state. Fortunately, however, not one photo of him or Conrad had been printed. The best way to get information, Tyler knew, was to remain undercover. Wanting to remain anonymous for as long as possible, he'd been careful to avoid reporters and had asked his twin brother to do the same. He'd even slipped by Walter's secretary when he'd visited the office, demanding answers from the notorious gem dealer.

My father. Even unspoken, the words left a sour taste on his tongue. But even stronger than the bitterness he felt was his need for vengeance. Walter was the reason he'd relocated to San Francisco. Although Tyler hadn't been officially assigned to his father's case, he continued to work with the prosecution. He knew he wouldn't be satisfied until he saw Walter tried, convicted and locked away for life.

Sara sat on the couch, applying the damp paper towels to Linda's forehead. "I'm going to have a talk with Walter," she said, gently stroking Linda's brow. "It's obvious he's been working this girl too hard… Oh, good, I think she's coming around. You'd better go, Tyler. The first person she sees when she wakes up should be someone she knows."

So. Lyla Sinclair was Linda Mailer, and she worked for Walter. Except she wasn't just his accountant, she was his spy. Walter knew about the ongoing investigation, but he had no idea what or how much the D.A. had on him. He wanted information and was probably paying Lyla—Linda—a bonus for her extracurricular activities.

It made sense. Hiring a private investigator to look into D.A. matters would have been too risky. Why should Walter trust an outsider when he had other options?

Why, that little tramp… She'd deliberately sought him out. Followed him that night to the hotel. He felt a small smile pull at his lips. Apparently, she'd had no qualms about mixing business with pleasure. He didn't know if spending the night with him had been planned from the start, but one thing he was sure of—she'd wanted him.

He tried to recollect how much he might have disclosed that night. Funny how he could remember what she wore, how she smelled, how her skin felt under his touch. But no words came to mind.

And then it all came back. He cringed inwardly, but his reaction had nothing to do with the case. When he recalled what he'd done, the sappy things he'd said…

He forced himself back to the present. This was the

first time he'd ever been in a ladies' room, and he was more than a little uncomfortable. Nevertheless, wild horses couldn't drag him away. He had to get to the bottom of this. "I'm not going anywhere."

There was no doubt in his mind that Sara found his behavior bizarre. "Then wait over there," she said, pointing to the alcove behind the couch near the doorway. "She doesn't know you. I don't want her to be frightened." As if on cue, Linda moaned, and Tyler reluctantly moved across the room.

Sara turned her attention back to Linda. "Open your eyes," she gently coaxed. "Are you all right?"

Why is that the first thing people ask when someone who has fainted awakens? Tyler wondered. Jeez, did she look all right? He knew she couldn't see him from her reclining position, but he could see her over the back of the couch. Even from where he stood, he could see she was paler than the moon in daylight.

His eyes roamed across her body, which seemed lost in that awful sack she was wearing. Hard to believe she was the same woman who had enticed him, the same woman who had led him by the hand to the registrar's desk and then watched eagerly as he signed them in.

Mr. and Mrs. John Smith.

Alias Lyla and Thomas.

"Thomas," she said, her voice barely a gasp.

He made a move to approach her, but Sara shot him a warning glance.

He was tired of playing the waiting game. He'd been patient far too long about a lot of things, but all that was about to change. It was payback time.

She'd played him for a fool, but this was just the first

round. This was a game she had no chance of winning. After all, who was the pro here? True, she'd managed to deceive him and then he hadn't been able to find her, but hell, he hadn't been made a detective for no good reason. At only twenty-four, he'd been the youngest cop in Colorado to get his gold shield.

Oh, yeah, things were about to change. Before he was through with her, he'd have all the information he needed to have Walter locked away.

When Linda tried to sit up, the room swirled around her. She fell back against the couch. "Wh-where am I?"

"Don't try to move," Sara said. "Wait until the dizziness subsides."

"You don't understand. Gun…have to warn them…"

"Gun?" Sara repeated. "Linda, what are you talking about?"

"That man—he was coming in our direction. He's here to kill Walter!"

Sara sighed with what seemed to be relief. "Sweetie, no one's going to kill Walter. Walter's not even here."

Linda took a deep breath. "The killer doesn't know that! He's got a gun, I tell you. I saw him go for it! He's a hired killer! What if he just starts shooting? You've got to call the police!"

"Listen to what you're saying, sweetheart. Hired killers don't just go around shooting at random. You're just a little confused. The man who was coming over to us is Tyler, Conrad's brother. He's not a criminal, he's a cop." Sara looked up and shook her head, as though gesturing to someone, then turned back to Linda. "He wasn't going for his gun, he was undoing his jacket. It was too warm in there. It must have been the heat that caused you to faint. I was feeling a little woozy myself. Believe me, I intend to speak to the management about this. Just because it's October doesn't mean they have to pump up the heat. With so many people here at the party, it's like a furnace in that room."

Linda's head was whirling. A cop? Thomas was a cop?

Thomas was Tyler?

No wonder she had mistaken Conrad for Thomas. Tall and muscular, both twins had the same dark hair, the same green eyes, the same cocky smile. Yet though they were identical twins, there was something different about Tyler. It was something unique, something that had attracted her the night they'd met.

"No gun?" she asked in a weak voice.

"No gun. Not an illegal gun, that is. Tyler is a detective with the San Francisco Police Department."

Linda groaned. "I feel so stupid."

"No, you mustn't feel that way. You're not well. People often get confused when they're sick."

"I'm not sick. I—" Linda bit down on her lip.

"What is it?" When Linda didn't answer, Sara gently prodded, "I'd like to think we're friends, Linda. You can talk to me about anything."

Why not? Linda thought. Her little secret wasn't one she could keep for long. Aside from Sadie, no one else knew. She might as well let the cat out of the bag, and this was as good a time as any.

"I'm two months pregnant," she blurted.

At first, Sara looked stunned. Then, once again she raised her head and glanced behind the couch. She made a dismissive gesture with her hand, then smiled brightly at Linda. "My, you're full of surprises! I didn't even know you were seeing anyone! I have to say, this party is turning into quite a night. It was originally intended as a welcoming party for Tyler and Conrad. Then, just before you arrived, Emily and Lazhar announced that they were expecting. And now you say you're expecting, too. Wouldn't it be something if you and Emily shared the same due date?"

Linda couldn't reply. The lump in her throat felt as large as a golf ball.

"Oh," Sara said flatly. "Me and my big mouth. You're not happy about this." She took Linda's hand. "Listen to me. I want you to know you're not alone. You're going to have to make some decisions, but remember, whatever you decide, you have friends, and we'll help in any way we can."

"I'm not going to have an abortion, if that's what you mean," Linda snapped.

"I was talking about your life in general," Sara said softly.

Her mouth trembling, Linda fought back tears. "I'm sorry. I didn't mean to snarl at you. I just don't know how this could have happened. I don't usually…I never…" She let her voice trail off.

Contrary to what Sara might think, Linda didn't have many friends. But Sara was right about one thing. Linda had some decisions to make, and soon. Though not about having the baby. She intended to have this baby, and she intended to raise it alone. She was more concerned with the practical issues. She earned a decent salary working for Walter, but San

Francisco was an expensive place to live. She could support herself just fine, but could she support a child? Yet she didn't want to leave the city. Here, she'd finally found some peace of mind. Here, she'd begun to heal.

Here, she had Walter, whom she trusted and respected, and here, she had Sadie, whom she had known since the third grade. These days, Sadie was understandably preoccupied with her upcoming wedding, but Linda knew that even after Sadie was married, they would always be friends.

Aside from the financial aspect, something else worried her, as well. What about Tyler? Would he demand a say in his child's life? She didn't want him as a role model for her child. Maybe the man she'd slept with wasn't a cold-blooded killer, but he was still a liar and a sleaze. Everyone knew why he had moved to San Francisco. It was no secret. He was trying to gather enough evidence to have Walter indicted. She was sure he'd sought her out only to obtain information. Why else would he have given her the time of day? Why else had he lied to her about his identity? If she never laid eyes on him again, it would be too soon.

Of course, her lying to him about her own identity was an entirely different matter.

"What about the father?" Sara asked, as though reading Linda's mind. She didn't ask who he was, but Linda could tell she was curious.

Sara continued to make strange gestures at something—or someone—behind the couch. "What on earth is going on?" Linda asked. She sat up and looked behind her. Once again she was overcome with dizziness, but this time it had nothing to do with the pregnancy. Tyler had overheard everything she'd said.

Over the buzzing in her ears, she heard Sara say, "I'm so sorry, Linda. I tried to get him to leave, but he wouldn't budge. But don't worry. He's family. You can trust him."

Linda was afraid that the look on Tyler's face would give him away. It didn't take more than a second. Sara had learned the answer to the question she'd held back. The astonishment in her eyes confirmed it.

Chapter Two

Just what kind of game was she playing? He rounded the couch and reached for her arm. "Get your purse, *Lyla*. We're leaving."

"Tyler, stop it!" Sara said, grabbing his wrist. "What's the matter with you? Can't you see she's not feeling well? Settle down, take a breather. Then we'll discuss this like adults. You two need to talk, but in a calm, rational way."

"You got that right," he growled. "'You two' meaning me and my father's sneaky accountant. Leave us alone, Sara."

She looked at Linda's drawn face. "I'm not going anywhere," she said with the same resolution Tyler had shown only minutes ago.

"In that case, we are." He bent low and, as he'd done earlier in the banquet room, gathered Linda in his arms.

"I'm taking her out of here. Make our apologies to the guests."

"I'm pregnant, not helpless," Linda piped up in a small voice. "I'd appreciate it if you'd put me down. Please."

She'd appreciate it? Please? Her Pollyanna act didn't fool him for a minute. For one thing, Pollyanna didn't have a body like hers. That dress she had on might be shapeless and oversize, but the fabric was thin. He could feel almost every curve underneath, and what he couldn't feel, his memory supplied.

Damn straight she wasn't helpless. She knew exactly what she was doing. She pressed her body against his, all the while looking up at him with those big, brown eyes.

She knew the effect she had on him. It was the same effect she'd had on him that night at the hotel, when he'd first seen her with her friend at a table by the bar. Two months ago, she'd played him for a sucker, but it was a role he had no intention of repeating. He was sure she was up to something. She was no more pregnant than he was.

"I'm a little cold now," she said in a pouting voice. "Did someone turn down the heat? If we're going out, I'll need to get my coat. I can't possibly leave without it." She wriggled against him, her breasts pushing against his arm.

In spite of himself, desire kicked in as though on automatic pilot. She thought someone had turned down the heat? To him, the ladies' lounge was fast becoming a steam room.

But she was right about one thing. She'd need her

coat. The coastal night air would be chilly. Reluctantly, he set her down, worried that she would bolt. He remembered how he'd felt the morning after they'd made love, when he'd awakened and discovered she was gone.

"You can get your coat from Sara later," he said, removing his sports jacket. "This should keep you warm." He slid his jacket over her shoulders, accidentally brushing his hand against her cheek. He pulled back quickly, as though he'd received an electric shock.

"The paramedics are probably on the way," Sara said to Linda. "You should let them look you over. You're still shaky."

"I'll be fine," Linda said, pulling the jacket closed. She smiled weakly at Sara. "Don't worry. I want to go with him, really."

Cupping Linda's elbow, Tyler led her through the parking lot. He unlocked his car with his remote, then walked to the passenger side and opened the door.

She didn't move. "I've changed my mind. I'm not going anywhere with you. I'm going home."

"You're in no condition to drive. What if you get dizzy?" When she didn't answer, he let out an exasperated breath. "What do you think is going to happen? Sara saw us leave together. She's a witness. Now get in before I pick you up again and dump you inside."

"What about my car? I'm parked on the other side of the lot."

"Forget about your car. We'll get it later. For Chrissake, get in."

"I would appreciate it if you didn't swear."

"Dammit, Linda—"

She stood next to the car, hands on hips, the look on her face warning him that she meant business. "I'm only getting in if you promise to tone down your language."

First, she practically accuses him of being a kidnapper, and then, she reproaches him for his language? The woman was nuts. Or maybe not. Maybe this was part of her act. Maybe she'd even staged her fainting spell. After all, she was a liar. Lyla, she'd said her name was. Lyla from Wisconsin.

"You wouldn't know a promise if it hit you in the face," he said, growing impatient. "Keeping a promise takes integrity, and you're the last person who should be talking about integrity."

"What about you, Mr. Thomas McMann?"

He had no intention of discussing ethics standing in a parking lot. "Look, are you getting in or not?"

She cast him a stony look, then climbed into the car. "Fine. But I'm only going with you because Sara was right. We need to talk."

He pulled out of the lot, the tires of his car screeching in protest. He and Linda needed to talk, all right. In a calm, rational way, Sara had said. Except what he was feeling was neither calm nor rational. How was he supposed to remain calm when the woman sitting next him was claiming she was carrying his baby? As far as being rational, what about the way his breathing had become tight and painful just because he was near her? He could feel her eyes on him as they drove off. Dark liquid eyes that could turn a man to oatmeal.

Get a grip, he ordered himself. The woman you made love to doesn't exist.

"Can you slow down, please?" she asked sweetly. "I wouldn't want you to have an accident."

He glanced at her with disdain. On the surface she was all sugar; on the inside she was cyanide. She was the type who made a show of how she preferred to see a half-empty glass as half-full. The type who was careful not to say a bad word about anyone. The type who stuck a knife in you as soon as you turned your back.

He pressed down on the accelerator, swearing under his breath.

She turned her head and stared out the window.

Moments later, he pulled off the road. He turned off the ignition, then came around to her side and opened her door. "We're here. Get out."

"Where's here?" she asked in a timorous voice.

He had to hand it to her, she was good. For a moment he almost believed she was afraid. "Baker Beach. We're going for a walk."

She looked around furtively, like a fawn searching for its mother, and then rested her eyes on his face. "I don't think this is a good idea. It's nighttime. It's so…dark."

Aw, hell. How could he stay angry when she kept looking at him that way? If he had any brains, he'd arrest her on the spot. Eyes like those were lethal. "It's not that dark," he said gruffly, taking her hand. "There's a full moon, and look at those stars. This has become one of my favorite spots. I come here whenever I have something to mull over." Something meaning his vendetta against the man who buttered her bread, but this he didn't mention. The last thing he wanted to do was discuss Walter. "Look over on your left. The view of the Golden Gate Bridge is spectacular."

"True, it is pretty here. But is it safe?"

Soft and small, her hand felt just as he remembered. Her hand in his as he'd led her from the table, into the lobby of the hotel…

"I'm a cop, remember? I won't let anything happen."

That seemed to do it, because she got out of the car. She crouched low to remove her shoes, her dress lifting well above her knees. Her hands weren't all he remembered with clarity. Those legs, long and willowy, wrapped around his waist…

"There now," she said, springing upright. "We wouldn't want to ruin our shoes, now would we? What about you, Tyler?"

His gaze traveled past the bridge, where the rugged rocky cliffs wound across the terrain. "I'm fine," he mumbled. But he wasn't fine, and it wasn't his feet he was worried about. Focus, he ordered himself. Find out what she's after.

"Listen to that roar," she said when they'd reached the shoreline. "The undertow must be pretty strong."

"You sound as if you know this beach. Not that I'm surprised. This is the nude area."

She assumed her hands-on-hips, schoolmarm pose. "Tyler, stop it right now. Why must you be so vituperative?"

Vituperative? Hell, he didn't even know what it meant. She must have read his confusion, because she clarified, "There's no call to be insulting. Anyway, you're supposed to be the moody twin, not the rude one. Although," she added, her mouth in a pout, "I can understand why you're upset. You regret spending the night with someone like me."

Something in her tone arrested him. Or maybe it was the way the moonlight played with the many shades of red in her hair, or the way the beating of his heart drummed out the roar of the ocean. "Let's get something straight. I don't regret that night. What makes you think I'm sorry?"

Shoot, why had he gone and said that? He was full of regrets, all right. The woman spelled trouble, and woman trouble was the last thing he needed. He had to remain focused, clear. He couldn't allow anything to interfere with his plans.

His mission, he called it. Yet he knew it was more than that. Somewhere along the way, he'd turned his mother's deathbed wish for revenge into a personal crusade.

"Let's face it, I'm not exactly your type," Linda said, picking at an imaginary thread on her dress.

Good thing they were at a beach. If she wanted to fish, this was the place. "Yeah? What type is that?"

"You're right, it's beautiful out here," she answered, evading his question.

Maybe she was trying to tell him that he wasn't *her* type.

She raised her head, and he could swear he saw that look in her eyes. It was the look she'd given him the night they'd met. The look that said she knew he wanted her, and that the feeling was mutual. Before he realized what he was doing, he pulled her to him, crushing her against his chest, enveloping her in his arms. She let out a breathless gasp, which he quickly silenced when he pressed his lips to hers.

Her knees must have buckled, or maybe he was the one to buckle, he wasn't quite sure. It was as if a force stronger than gravity was pulling them down, and in the next instant they were on the sand, arms and legs tangled, their bodies locked together. His lips never left hers. He pushed his tongue in deeper, eager to rediscover what he'd been fantasizing about these past two months, eager to reclaim what he'd believed he'd lost.

She didn't try to stop him. Didn't try to break the kiss.

And then her body went limp.

She turned her head away.

Well, that answered *that*. Apparently, he wasn't her type, after all. His thoughts returned to the night they'd made love, only this time the memory left him feeling cold. Obviously, she hadn't been as swept away as she'd led him to believe. So much with her mixing business with pleasure. It had all been an act.

They pulled to a sitting position. "I'm sorry," she mumbled, adjusting her glasses. "You're angry, I can tell. I don't blame you. It's just that…I can't…" She lowered her gaze.

He was the one who'd been out of line, and she was apologizing? Enough, he told himself. She was up to something, and he aimed to find out what it was. "Let's get out of here," he said sourly, rising to his feet. He extended his hand. "Take it," he growled when she just sat there. "I wouldn't want you to fall and hurt the baby. If there *is* a baby."

"What's that supposed to mean?"

"Oh, come on. I don't know what you think you're doing, but trust me, I'll figure it out. You work for Walter. That itself is proof you're up to no good."

She scrambled to her feet, dusting the sand from her dress. "He's just trying to run a business. Why is it whenever someone is successful, the rest of the world feels it's their moral duty to bring him down? Maybe if you'd take the time to get to know him, you'd realize he's a decent, caring man."

"Get to know him!" Tyler spat. "He won't even acknowledge that I'm alive. Simple, you call him. That's a laugh. Devious would be a more apt description. Did you say decent? Now that's more than a laugh. It's a bad joke. A bad joke that needs to be put to rest once and for all."

"And you'll do anything it takes, including sleeping with his accountant to get information." She picked up her shoes and, pushing past him, headed back to where they were parked.

"Let's get one thing straight," he said, scrambling after her. "I didn't know who you were that night in the lounge. I was there on official business, on a case that had nothing to do with Walter. I was about to call it a night and go home, when you approached me. You were the one who sought *me* out."

"Sought you out! Why you egotistical, self-centered boor! Tell me something, Mr. First-Class Detective, why on earth would I do that?"

"You tell me. You're the one working for Parks. From what I hear, the two of you are pretty tight. What else do you do for him?"

"Why you—" She raised her hand to slap him, then abruptly dropped it. "That question doesn't deserve a response. And I don't believe in violence."

"Glad to know it. I wouldn't want you to get physical. But I was talking about spying, darlin', nothing else. How much is the old man paying you to do his dirty work? Well, you can tell him to save his money. In fact, you can tell him we've almost got enough evidence to make an arrest, and what we have is solid."

"Almost? Now that's the key word, isn't it? But almost won't cut it. It's like the lottery. Either you win or you don't. Almost won't pay the bills. You're never going to indict him, and do you know why? You don't have any real proof. All the evidence is circumstantial. It's not concrete, or you would have arrested him by now. No, you're the spy here. You're the one who went on the prowl, looking for me. You're…oh, no, not again."

"What?" he asked.

"Morning…sickness," she sputtered. "I think…I'm going…to be sick."

He couldn't decide what was worse, a woman feeling nothing or getting nauseous after he had kissed her.

Morning sickness, she'd said. As in pregnant. Something didn't add up. What did her spying on him have to do with her claiming to be pregnant?

Instinctively, he shifted into investigative mode. The results of the paternity suit against Walter had been made public last month. What if, after learning that Walter was his father, she'd thought she'd seen a way to get a piece of the Parks fortune? She'd already slept with Walter's son; the timing would be right.

Seemed like paternity claims were in style these days, he thought wryly. Except that unlike his, hers was phony. Not only that, apparently she hadn't thought the whole thing through. How would she explain her situation seven months from now? Unless she wasn't planning to. Unless she intended to leave town long before then, with a heavy chunk of payoff cash in her suitcase. But his theory still had holes. Wouldn't she know he'd insist she see a doctor to confirm her allegation?

"Come on," he said roughly. "I'm taking you back to your car."

By the water, her face had appeared even paler than it had in the restaurant, but as they approached the car, in the dim light from the street lamp she looked almost green.

Immediately, he felt chastened. She really *was* sick. Maybe her fainting in the restaurant hadn't been an act. For the first time that evening, the possibility that she really might be pregnant entered his head.

Two questions assailed him at once. What if the baby was his? What if it wasn't?

The thought of her with another man made him crazy. Which made him even crazier. What did he care? It wasn't as if there was anything between them.

She began to sway, and instantly he was jarred from his musing. "Lean against me," he said. "Take deep, slow breaths. There you go. That's it. Slowly. You'll be okay."

She did as he said, not resisting when he wrapped his arm around her shoulder. A moment later, she looked up at him and said, "Thank you, Tyler. I feel much better." She gave him a weak smile. "You know, you're not as hard-boiled as you make yourself out to be. Underneath that rough exterior, there's a nice guy. You should let him out more often."

"And you should get some rest. I'll take you to your car tomorrow. Right now, I'm driving you home. You live in Noe Valley, right?"

She stared at him. "How did you know?"

He knew a lot more than that. Robert Jackson, the prosecutor assigned to the case, had done his homework. A file existed for anyone who had ever been associated with Walter.

"I guess Sara must have told you," she said before he could reply, and he didn't correct her. "But I'm fine, really. Take me back to the restaurant. I can drive myself home."

She didn't look fine. "No arguments. You have to think of the baby." He helped her into the car and then went around to the driver's side. The baby, he repeated to himself. But whose baby? It suddenly dawned on him that she hadn't actually said he was the father.

"I still can't believe that Thomas is you," she said as he pulled onto the road. "You realize what this means, don't you? Walter is the baby's grandfather. I can't imagine anything more wonderful."

So. She was saying that Tyler *was* the father. He suppressed a derisive laugh. It was almost ironic. He might not have inherited his father's name, but if what she was saying was true, he'd inherited one of Walter's traits. One of Walter's less admirable traits, he thought with self-loathing. Like his father, Tyler, it seemed, had a penchant for creating bastards.

But what if she was lying? She'd lied to him the night they met; why should he believe anything she told him now? He eyed her critically. That smock she had on was deceptive. Two months, she'd said. Maybe she was a little more pregnant than she claimed.

Maybe now that she knew who Tyler was, she thought she could cash in. Maybe she figured she could do a lot worse than marrying the head honcho's son. Why settle for kiss-off money when you thought you could get your hands on the whole enchilada?

She prattled on with her nauseating tribute. "I know you two don't get along, but I feel confident that in time you'll come to some sort of understanding. Once you get to know him, I'm sure you'll realize what a good man he really is."

Tyler wished he'd worn boots. He was wading in something, and it wasn't Bay water.

But what if the baby *was* his? Walter might be the paternal grandfather, but Tyler would see him in hell before he allowed him into his child's life.

This can't be happening, he thought, his head pounding. He'd never wanted a family, and since discovering the truth about who he was, his resolve had been reinforced. Any child he fathered would be descended from that monster. "I want you to have a blood test."

A silence moved through the air, as thick as the fog that was now swirling past the car windows. "They're not always accurate," she finally answered, her tone icy. "Why not do DNA testing instead? You seem to have *that* science down to an art."

"Now wait a minute," he said, striving to keep his voice steady. "I did what I had to do. I never doubted my mother's story for a minute, but I had to have legal proof that Walter is my father. I need all the evidence I can get to put him away."

Damn. He said he wasn't going to go there. Wasn't going to get into a discussion about Walter. But she had a way about her. He couldn't put his finger on it, but something about her made him want to explain himself. Made him want to seek her approval.

"Do you realize the embarrassment you've caused?" she hurled at him. "What does his paternity have anything to do with the embezzling charge? Eventually the charges against him will be dropped, but people will remember the scandal forever. Did you have to go public?"

"Hey, I wasn't the one who released the story to the papers. Not that this is the sort of thing that can be kept quiet for long."

Why was he defending himself? He wasn't the one under investigation. He wasn't the one who would be arrested for fraud and embezzlement.

He wasn't the one who would be tried and convicted for the murder of Jeremy Carlton.

In spite of his resolve to remain calm, he felt his anger rising. "Do you really believe I give a rat's tail about Walter's embarrassment? He cheated the man I believed was my father. He destroyed everything. The business, the family, my *mother*—" He stopped abruptly. Granted, his accusations were no longer a secret, but he had to watch what he said. Even if she hadn't sought him out that night to obtain information, even if their meeting had been an act of fate, she worked for Walter. Moreover, it was clear that the relationship went beyond the office. Her approval be damned; he couldn't risk revealing something Walter didn't know. "So you're saying you refuse to have the baby tested?" he asked.

"What I'm saying is that it makes no difference whether or not you're the father."

Once again he was filled with jealousy. "Are you saying I'm not?"

"You're not listening, Tyler. I'm saying it's irrelevant, since I intend to raise this baby by myself."

Was this her angle? Some sort of reverse psychology? Was this where he was supposed to get down on his knees and beg her to marry him? Well, he wasn't falling for it. If she thought she could marry her way into Walter's fortune, she had another think coming. Even if the courts ruled that Tyler was entitled to a share of the Parks fortune, he wouldn't go within an inch of that money. As far as he was concerned, it was dirty money, tainted by Walter's greedy hands.

"Walter's money has nothing to do with me," he said. "If I agreed to marry you, you wouldn't see a dime."

She let out a scornful laugh. "What makes you think I'd consider marrying you? It can't be the sex. I have news for you, it wasn't that good."

Spoken like the ice queen she was. He felt as if he'd been slapped.

And she'd accused *him* of being vituperative.

She unlocked the front door to her building, angry tears escaping down her cheeks. Stop it, she ordered herself. He can't touch you now.

If she agreed to marry him? Who did he think he was? And then to imply that she was after the Parks fortune! What gall. She could still hear his words, as though he were right there, standing beside her.

She could still feel his body crushing against hers as they tumbled to the sand…

She listened to the roar of the engine as he sped off

into the night, then quickly glanced inside the building. Good. All clear. No one was in the entranceway. No one to notice if she let go and cried.

No one lurking in the shadows, ready to pounce.

She hoped Sadie was home. She hated coming back to an empty apartment. Since becoming engaged, Sadie spent most nights at her fiancé's apartment. Next week, the situation would become permanent.

Although Linda was sorry that Sadie was leaving, she was genuinely happy for her friend. Sadie had known she wanted to be Frank's wife the first time she'd laid eyes on him, two years ago at a party. But now Linda had a problem. She'd been looking for a new roommate for weeks, to no avail. You're too picky, Sadie had accused. How can you tell what someone's like after just one meeting?

Linda knew that if she didn't find someone soon, she would have to move. Together, she and Sadie could afford the rent on the two-bedroom apartment, but on one income, it would be impossible. Then there was the baby. Raising a child in a two-parent household was expensive enough; she couldn't even imagine how she would manage doing it on her own.

Nevertheless, she didn't want to move. She liked living here. Where else would she find an apartment as perfect?

Situated in the trendy Noe Valley, the large two-story Victorian structure had been converted into a four-unit apartment complex in the early 1970s. Centrally located on a lovely tree-lined street, the building was just a short distance from 24th Street with its many shops and cafés. But this, for Linda, wasn't its main attraction.

Living here, amidst an old-world charm, she felt a kind of peace, as though she could shut out all the evil in the world just by closing her door.

She looked up at the video camera suspended from the ceiling. She knew that if there was any kind of commotion, or if the camera went dead, a police car would arrive within minutes. This added security was another reason she'd let Sadie talk her into taking the apartment in spite of the high rent.

She had to find a roommate fast, and not just because she needed someone to share expenses. She hated living alone.

Almost there now, she thought as she scurried upstairs. She felt herself relax.

But then Tyler's face rose in her mind, and her pulse skittered erratically. She didn't want to dwell on what had happened on the beach, but she couldn't stop the images from forming in her head. For one brief moment when he'd kissed her, she'd lost herself in his arms. Just as she'd done that night two months ago, she'd allowed herself to *feel*. She couldn't let that happen again. She couldn't allow herself to lose control.

When you lose control, someone gets hurt.

She couldn't believe the things she'd said to him. Usually when confronted, she became tongue-tied. But not this time. This time, she'd lashed back. She pictured the look on his face when, after he'd accused her of going after the Parks fortune, she'd attacked his masculinity. No man wanted to hear that he was a dud in bed. She hadn't said it in quite those words, but the meaning had been clear. Clear but not true, she thought, recalling that night in August. She felt her cheeks grow hot. Oh, so not true.

At first, after she'd spoken the words, he'd looked startled, even angry, but then his expression changed. Something in his eyes told her it was more than his pride she'd wounded. She'd recognized in his eyes a vulnerability that she often felt herself.

Wouldn't you know it, she thought, dismayed. The one time I speak up, I say the wrong thing. True, she'd wanted to lash out, but she hadn't wanted to hurt him. She didn't want to hurt anyone.

When she opened the door to her apartment, the noise from the TV in the living room assaulted her. She sighed with relief. Sadie was home.

Chapter Three

"That scumbag! I wondered why you were home so early."

Sadie poured herself a cup of coffee and joined Linda at the table. The tiny but cheerful kitchen was where they liked to talk things over, sometimes laughing, other times solemn, but always fortified with a plate of cookies. Linda was the first to admit she didn't like cooking, but baking was another matter. She loved the smell of fresh-baked goods, especially chocolate chip cookies. It reminded her of the kind of home she'd always dreamed of.

"It was just awful. I can't believe the things he said." Or the things I said, Linda thought, heat stealing into her cheeks.

"What about the drive home? That couldn't have been pleasant."

"Oh, he tried to make small talk—you know how much I love that—but I couldn't even look at him. Then he put in a CD and that was the end of it."

But that hadn't been the end of it. She'd wanted to yell, cry, throw something, but she'd just sat there, feeling claustrophobic next to him in the car. Tyler was already under the impression she was a little off-kilter. What would he have thought if she'd had a full-blown anxiety attack?

The events of the evening replayed in her head, causing her to groan inwardly. First, she saw him approaching in the restaurant, and then she fainted dead away. Later, she agreed to talk with him and then rebuked him for his language. And let's not leave out what happened on the beach, she reminded herself. As if she could forget. After she let him kiss her, she pushed him away. No, not pushed him. She'd just lain there on the sand, as limp as a wet noodle.

A little off-kilter? He probably thought she was certifiable.

"Drink up," Sadie said, motioning to Linda's glass. "It's good for the baby, and it'll calm your nerves."

"Yuck. I hate milk, especially warm milk. But I suppose I'll have to give up the good stuff now that I'm pregnant."

"As if you were ever a drinker." Sadie's brow creased. "I would never have left you that night if I'd thought you'd had too much to drink. You know that, don't you?"

"I told you, I only had one glass of wine," Linda reassured her, wishing it hadn't been the case. If she'd had too much to drink, she might have had an excuse for what she'd done. Not a good excuse, but an excuse nonetheless. "Besides," she said, eyeing her friend's cup, "I was talking about coffee just now. That's 'the good stuff.' Not that I'd call what you're drinking 'good.' I never did understand the reason for decaf."

"And I was talking about friendship." Sadie's face was wrenched with guilt. "This is all my fault. Some friend I was, leaving you alone in a bar."

"I wasn't alone, remember?"

"My point exactly. We should have driven home together that night, just as we'd planned."

Linda regarded her with exasperation. "Will you please lose that pained expression? You're not to blame. How could you know that I'd leave with someone I'd just met? *I* didn't even know. Sleeping with strangers isn't exactly a habit of mine." That was an understatement. Even dating wasn't on her list of preferred things to do.

She pictured Tyler's face, the way his gaze had swept over her with frank appreciation. For one brief night she'd been able to forget that she was Linda Mailer. She'd even believed him when he told her she was beautiful. All he'd had to do was whisper that he wanted her, and the next instant she'd found herself in his arms, riding the elevator up to a room.

"I shouldn't have let Frank come pick me up," Sadie pressed on. "When he called me on my cell to tell me his flight had been canceled, I should have told him I'd see him in the morning. I swear, that man lives out of a suitcase. I must be demented, marrying a pilot."

"You're all talk, Sadie Heath. You know you love him more than anything in the world."

"Oh, I'm demented all right. I should have realized right away that Thomas would bring grief. I should never have left you alone with that scumbag."

"Tyler. His name is Tyler, remember? And will you please stop calling him a scumbag? I hate that word."

Sadie gave her a sideways glance. "If I didn't know better, I'd say you have a thing for this guy. Now listen up, honey. The man lied to you, and in my book, any man who lies is a scumbag. You can't imagine how many times I hear stories like this at the salon. Sometimes the men in these sad tales are married. Sometimes they're just plain mean. But the one thing they all have in common is that they're liars, every one of them."

"He's a detective on the force. He probably wanted to be sure of me before revealing his identity."

There's something I have to tell you, Linda recalled him saying the night they'd met. Would he have told her if she hadn't stopped him? Would she have revealed her own identity?

Sadie narrowed her eyes. "Are you saying you're good enough to share his bed but not good enough to know who he is? Sorry, I don't buy his I'm-a-detective excuse for a minute. You're not a suspect in one of his cases. What sort of man acts like that?"

"A man who's been hurt," Linda answered. "A man with a grudge. Tyler's made Walter his scapegoat. He blames him for all the Carltons' troubles."

"It's more than a grudge," Sadie insisted. "It's blood-thirsty vengeance. You read the newspapers. And your office must be buzzing with gossip. Tyler won't give up until he sees Walter in prison, and he's the type who'll stop at nothing to get what he wants." She snorted. "Once a liar, always a liar."

Linda's patience was quickly vanishing. "You seem to forget I lied that night, too. Remember Lyla, *Sandra?*"

Sadie scowled at that. "You told me that the only way you'd come out with me was if we both used fake names. Not only did I lie, I felt like a thief in the night. I had to run off the moment I saw Frank in the doorway, because I was afraid he would spill the beans."

"All I'm saying is that sometimes people have to hide the truth. Sometimes they have a reason. Even you went along with it."

"Just because I went along with it doesn't make it right. I never understood why you wanted to lie in the first place."

"Don't you see? It wasn't really me that night," Linda persisted. "You turned me into someone else, and I needed a name to go with my new persona. It was all a fantasy." But the fantasy had developed into something real. Her pregnancy was a testament to that.

Sadie shrugged. "I thought a change would be good for you. I'm not just talking about the clothes and the makeup. I'm talking about the way you feel about yourself. I thought that getting all dolled up would give you a shot of confidence." She rested her gaze on Linda's dress. "While we're on the subject of clothes, where on earth did you find that smock?"

Linda sighed. "This is me. This is how I dress. I'm not you, Sadie."

"And thank the Lord for that. Somehow I don't think big blond hair would suit you," Sadie joked.

One thing about Sadie, she could lighten any mood. At the moment, however, Linda was in no mood for humor. "We don't even want the same things in life. Like marriage, for instance. I'm overjoyed for you, but it's not something I want for myself."

"We might want different things, but we both want to be happy. And you won't find happiness until you stop hiding."

"The pop psychologist speaks. Okay, I'll bite. How am I hiding?"

"For one thing, you're a beautiful woman, but you go out of your way to make yourself look dowdy." Sadie leaned in close and picked up a strand of Linda's hair. "You could use a trim. Maybe add a few highlights. Make that red really shine. And will you look at those nails!" she said as Linda reached for another cookie. "Your cuticles are out of control. Why don't you come by the salon next week? I'll give you the royal treatment. Facial, manicure, the whole works. I'll have Katrina do your hair. She's new, but you'll like her. She doesn't talk much."

Sadie was like a steamroller. Nothing stopped her. Even though sometimes Linda found it annoying, she had to admit that it was one of the qualities she admired most about her friend. It was this very persistence that had helped make *La Belle Coupe,* the beauty salon that Sadie owned and operated, the success it was. It was also this very persistence that had helped keep Linda from succumbing to depression after the accident.

"You never give up," Linda said, pushing the memory aside. The period after her sister had died was not something she liked to dwell on. "You're still trying to make me over. Can't you understand? I'm happy the way I am."

"Are you? Honey, my customers talk to me at the salon. No matter what I'm doing, whether I'm shampooing, coloring or blow-drying, if there's one thing I can spot, it's an unhappy woman. Usually she's unhappy because of something that happened a long time ago. Something in her past. But you've got to move on, I always say. You've got to get over it."

"Sadie…" Linda warned. They were heading into dangerous territory.

"Oh, I know. You want to leave the past buried. But that's just the problem. You're covering it up, like camouflage. I see this kind of thing all the time. Women come into the salon expecting me to perform miracles. I can cut their hair, dye it or perm it, but it always grows back the same. I can paint their nails or paint their faces, but it's only temporary. It doesn't last."

"Like a makeover," Linda said wryly. "Or a royal treatment at the salon."

Sadie wagged a finger. "There's nothing wrong with making yourself more attractive. If I believed there was, do you think I'd be in this business? You're not listening. I'm saying that if you've got problems, you've got to treat them, not just cover them up. Like dry hair. That's why we have conditioner. Or acne. You can't just hide it under a glob of foundation. You've got to treat it from within. Good nourishment and vitamins, that sort of thing."

"Is there a point to this?" Linda asked.

"You know what I'm going to say. I've said it to you before, and I'll keep saying it until it sinks in. Before you can put your demons to rest, before you can move on, you've got to confront them once and for all. You can't treat the soul until you acknowledge that it's ailing."

"That has to be the most convoluted reasoning I've ever heard," Linda scoffed. One thing, however, was clear. Sadie was worried about her. "I know you're just being a friend, and I appreciate it. If it hadn't been for you, I don't know how I would have survived after my sister died. But I'm okay now, and I've been okay for a long time."

Was she? Just less than an hour ago, sitting next to Tyler, she'd been worried about having an anxiety attack, even though she hadn't had one in years. But it had nothing to do with the past, as Sadie had suggested. It had been triggered by Tyler's despicable insinuations.

"I wasn't referring to the car accident," Sadie said softly. "I was referring to your mother."

Linda felt the color drain from her face. "You know what I think? I think you should save your pop psychology for your clients. I don't have to listen to this drivel."

She regretted her harsh tone the minute the words escaped her mouth. What was wrong with her? She wasn't the type who hurled insults. Normally she was the I-should-have-said type who thought of the exact thing to say after the fact, when she was alone, rehashing what had happened. But lately, she'd been throwing slurs like darts. She'd always believed that a snarky comeback would make her feel empowered, but she'd been wrong. All she felt was terrible. "I'm sorry, Sadie. I shouldn't have spoken to you that way. I know you're only trying to be helpful. You've always had my best interest at heart."

It was the truth. In the past, Sadie had been more than just helpful; she'd been a lifesaver. After Karen was killed in the car crash, Sadie had invited Linda to come out to California, where she'd lived since graduating from high school. Montana has too many bad memories, she'd said. You need a fresh start.

A fresh start, Linda repeated to herself. But now, according to Sadie, she needed to revisit the past. According to Sadie, Linda's spirit was far from healed.

"Oh, pooh," Sadie said. "If you can't throw a tantrum in front of your best friend, then she's not your best friend. Anyway, it's time I learned to keep my big mouth shut. 'Course I'd probably lose a lot of business. Those women don't come to me because they think I'm Vidal Sassoon. Not that I'm not as good," she added, a twinkle in her eye, "but to them I'm like a therapist. Only I cost a lot less, and they get a new look to boot." She took Linda's hands. "Seriously, honey, I know I've been busy with the wedding, but I want you to know you can come to me any time, with any problem. That's not going to change after I'm married. And I promise, no more world-according-to-Sadie lectures. The next time I stick my nose where it doesn't belong, you have my permission to stick my head under the dryer. In the meantime, if there's anything I can do, you just holler."

Linda rose from the table and carried her glass to the sink. "There *is* something you can do. Take me to the restaurant in the morning so I can get my car. Tyler said he'd take me, but I'm hoping he'll call first so I can tell him not to. I don't intend to see him again. This is *my* baby, and I don't want a man in my life telling me what to do." Not only were men controlling, they were undependable. She knew this for a fact. Her mother had told her, time and time again.

"Uh-huh," Sadie said in an infuriating way. "I think the lady doth protest too much. Seems to me— Oops, there I go again. Where's that hair dryer?"

Linda shook her head. "You're hopeless. Go ahead, say it. I know you're dying to. Something's on your mind, I can tell."

"Okay, since you asked. What about the jacket?"

"What jacket?"

"That snazzy blue sports jacket you hid in the closet the moment you entered the apartment. If you really didn't intend to see him again, you would have returned it before you left the car."

Linda rolled her eyes. "The pop psychologist speaks again. Are you saying I kept it on purpose so I could have an excuse to see him? What is this, high school? Well, you're wrong. I've told you over and over, I don't want a relationship. I'll never let a man get close to me."

Sadie chuckled. "Uh-huh. Honey, unless a star suddenly rises in the east, I'd say it's a little late."

Although it was only nine-thirty, Mike McGarret's, the popular sports bar where the precinct liked to hang out, was already bustling with activity. After greeting a few off-duty patrolmen at one of the jam-packed tables, Tyler threaded his way toward the bar. On the overhead big-screen TV, the Giants had just scored a run, and a loud cheer erupted.

"I didn't expect to see you here," Nick shouted over the clamor. "I take it that Parks showed up at the party."

Tyler slid onto a bar stool next to his friend at the

long mahogany bar. "That lowlife wouldn't dare show his mug," he grumbled after the noise had subsided. "Considerate of him, don't you think? Garbage like him would have stunk up the whole place."

Nick shot him a twisted smile. "Hey, if I'd known you'd be this much fun, I wouldn't have brought a date."

"You didn't," Tyler replied.

"The night is still young. It's Saturday, I'm off duty and I aim to please."

"Anyone in particular, or are you being hypothetical again?"

Joking around, watching the game, talking about women—this was what Tyler looked forward to at the end of a day. Later, he'd go home to his one-bedroom apartment where he could block out everything—job, friends, family, even his crusade against Walter. Mike McGarret's was where he unwound; his apartment was where he found refuge.

"A guy can dream," Nick said, raising his bottle in a mock salute to the leggy blonde at the end of the bar. He put down the bottle. "So what's eating you, Carlton? Aside from life, the universe and Parks. My guess is that the party was too rich for your taste. I'm not talking cuisine. I'm talking about the guest list."

Tyler signaled to the bartender and ordered a beer, then turned to Nick with amusement. "So now you're a mind reader?"

Nick tapped himself on the head. "Antennae, bud. It's what keeps us employed. A little intuition goes a long way in our line of work."

"Like I said, Walter wasn't there. Ergo, I had no qualms about the guest list. Emily, Lazhar, Cade…a person couldn't have better relatives even if he got to choose them himself." Too bad we don't get to choose our parents, he thought, but didn't say it. Some things didn't need to be spelled out. Between friends, some things were understood.

Not only was Nick Banning his partner, he was Tyler's best friend. It was no mystery why they'd clicked right off the bat when Tyler had joined the SFPD. When Nick was nine, his parents had been brutally killed. For years, he and his older brother, Mark, had been shuffled from one foster home to another. Like Nick, Tyler was a man with a troubled childhood. Feeling like an outcast was something they had in common.

"If it isn't the family that has you wound up, then what is it?" Nick asked. "Spill it, Carlton. Who is she?"

Either his partner's radar was in full operation, or Tyler was as transparent as the tape he used to lift fingerprints. "Linda Mailer," he replied. The bartender returned with a beer, and Tyler took a swallow. "Aka Lyla Sinclair." He debated mentioning the baby, but decided against it, at least until he'd figured out a plan of action.

"The woman from the hotel is Parks' accountant?" Nick let out a slow whistle. "Now that's convenient. She could be the answer to all your troubles."

Tyler knew what Nick meant. Get close to Linda, get close to Walter. Which was what he'd planned to do when he'd learned who she was. But he couldn't go through with it. He didn't use women to get what he wanted, information or otherwise. Not that spying hadn't crossed *her* mind.

He still wasn't convinced that she hadn't set out to milk him for information two months ago. The jury was still out on that one. Nevertheless, where Walter was concerned, one thing he was certain of. He and Linda were on opposite teams.

Opposites attract, he thought wryly. Maybe that was why he'd been drawn to her in the first place. "She's not the answer to all my troubles," he said. "She *is* trouble."

"Who, the virgin princess?"

Tyler stared at his friend. "I think you have the wrong fairy tale, pal. Aren't you forgetting one small detail? I spent the night with her."

Nick shook his head. "Which I find incredible. What's your secret, Carlton? You know what they call her down at the precinct. A cold fish. Everyone we questioned regarding the case says the same thing. All the guys she works with have asked her out, but she won't let any of them come within sneezing distance."

The ice queen, Tyler had thought earlier. His jaw clenched. "Just because a woman says no doesn't mean she's cold. If you have anything else to say about her that's not related to the case, I'd appreciate it if you kept it to yourself."

Nick raised his hands as though warding off a blow. "Hey, it didn't come from me. Besides, what do you care? It's not like you have a thing for her." When Tyler didn't answer, Nick grinned. "Oh, boy. The plot thickens. So that's why you've been searching for her. Here I thought you were looking for a lead in that gambling case, which is why you went to the hotel in the first place."

"You're nuts," Tyler said. "The woman means nothing to me."

"Right. Where have I heard that before? Every time

you start with someone new, it's the same old story. No, I take that back. You say it just before you're ready to call it quits."

"You're one to talk. I don't see you rushing to the altar."

"I'm working on it." He motioned to the end of the bar. "See that blonde? Who knows, she might be the future mother of my children. Mark my words, one of these days some woman is going to turn me into an honest man."

"I'll believe it when I see it," Tyler said, and took a swig of his beer. "Although you know my feelings on that particular subject."

"Yeah, I remember. In the line of fire, could get killed, not fair to our families…yada yada yada. I've heard it before. Here's a news flash. A meteor could fall out of the sky and wipe us out in the blink of an eye, but that doesn't mean I'm going to stop living. In fact, it supports what I've been saying all along. You have to live for today. And speaking of living," he said, tossing a five-dollar bill on the bar, "unlike someone else at this bar, I think I have a date. See you later, bud. Destiny awaits."

"Don't do anything I would," Tyler joked as Nick walked off. His partner was an enigma. On the one hand, he liked to stick to himself; on the other hand, he was a magnet for women.

Tyler finished his beer. He tried to watch the game on the screen, but he couldn't concentrate. He kept thinking about what Nick had said about living for today. But most people didn't make their living dealing with crime and danger. Most people planned for the future.

When Tyler had chosen to become a cop, he'd made the decision not to have kids. What if he were killed? He wouldn't want his children to grow up the way he had, without a father. He felt the same about marriage. He knew what loneliness could do to a woman. He had only to recall his mother's face.

But it was Elana's face, not his mother's, he pictured now. She'd once accused him of using his work as an excuse to avoid commitment. She'd even suggested that he'd chosen to become a cop to create this excuse. It wasn't true. As corny as it sounded, he'd always believed that good triumphed over evil and that justice must prevail. Elana had wanted marriage and kids, but he'd believed that the course he'd chosen excluded this. Eventually, they'd gone their separate ways.

Just as Nick had done earlier, Tyler raised his bottle in a silent salute. He hadn't thought about his high school sweetheart in a long time. After they'd split up, Tyler decided that relationships just weren't worth it. Too many expectations got shattered, too many hopes sucked down the drain. As for Elana, he'd heard she was married to a doctor, her third baby on the way.

Baby.

Dammit, the last thing he should be thinking of was a baby. As in family. As in marriage.

A baby deserved to have a father.

His mother used to talk about Jeremy in glowing terms, as though she could construct a father for her children out of mere words. To some extent it had worked. He wasn't the twins' biological father, and although he had existed only in their minds, he was the only father they had known.

But imagination was no substitute for the real thing. Tyler recalled the loneliness he'd felt while growing up, the acute sadness that had engulfed him whenever his friends went off with their dads. Hiking, bowling, fishing—the activity wasn't important. All he knew was that he was missing out.

If only he had one memory, one that was entirely his own. His mother had meant well, but Tyler knew that if given the opportunity, he'd trade all the hours he'd spent feeding his fantasy for one brief moment with the real thing.

His child deserved no less. And Tyler was convinced that the baby was his. He didn't know why he felt this way; it made no sense. Linda had lied the night they'd met, and she was nothing like the woman she'd pretended to be.

Maybe he believed it because of the way she'd reacted when he'd suggested she have a blood test. Indignant. Angry. Sure, it could have been an act, but how could she know he wouldn't insist? If the baby wasn't his, she had to know that he'd find out the truth.

Maybe it was because of male pride. Nick's words rang in his ears. The virgin princess, he'd called her. Cold. Those were labels bestowed by men who'd been turned down, labels men gave women who didn't sleep around. Maybe Linda was particular. Maybe she'd regarded Tyler as special.

Or maybe it was just his gut feeling. Antennae, Nick called it. It went a long way, on the job and off.

Suddenly Tyler didn't give a damn whether or not she was after the Parks fortune. All he cared about was the baby. He wanted his child to have a flesh-and-blood father, not some phantom built from dreams. Tyler could die in the line of duty, but any amount of time spent with his child, no matter how small, would be infinitely better than no time at all.

Maybe Nick was right. Maybe living for today was all anyone could expect.

Tyler considered ordering another beer. After the night he'd had, he figured he was entitled to some serious alcohol therapy. But drinking to forget his problems wasn't his style, and one drink was his limit when he knew he'd be driving. He didn't want to leave his car and take a taxi, since he planned on driving to Linda's place first thing in the morning. He had something to say to her, or more aptly, something to propose.

But there would be no ring, no kneeling, no imaginary violins playing in the background. He intended to present his offer like a business deal. She worked for Walter. She'd relate to that.

Of course, he didn't have to be unfriendly. A marriage of convenience didn't mean they couldn't enjoy a few fringe benefits. Her lovely lush lips appeared before him, the scent of her hair lingering in the air as though she were standing next to him.

He recalled the way her body had curled into his after they'd made love. With his arms around her in a protective embrace and her soft, silky hair sprayed across his pillow, they'd remained motionless, as though afraid to break the spell. After she'd fallen asleep, he'd lain beside her, still basking in the afterglow until he, too, drifted off to sleep, lulled by the gentle cadence of her breathing.

A heaviness centered in his chest. Going home to his empty apartment had suddenly lost its appeal.

Chapter Four

"Who in his right mind shows up unannounced at eight o'clock on a Sunday morning? Tell him I'm not home. No, don't. He'll never believe it. Tell him I'm still sleeping."

Sadie gawked at the face on the monitor. "You want me to send *that* away? Did getting pregnant make you blind? He's even more gorgeous than I remember. At least hear what he has to say before feeding him to the dogs."

Linda stared at her friend with amazement. "Are you sure you're the same person who called him a scumbag?"

"Let's just say I'm a forgiving person," Sadie answered, her eyes still glued to the screen. "But if you want him to leave, it's your call. Only tell him yourself. I'm not going to lie for you anymore."

"Traitor." But Linda knew that Sadie was right. It was time the lies stopped. "All right, I'll buzz him up.

It was optimistic of me, anyway, thinking I wouldn't have to face him. I'll give him his jacket, then tell him to leave. I have no desire to talk to him."

"Uh-huh," Sadie said, smiling in a knowing way.

A moment later, Tyler stood in the doorway of the apartment, looking casually handsome in a crewneck sweater and jeans. "Great security system," he said, glancing at the screen in the wall. "I'm impressed."

"Lots of little nooks in these old houses," Sadie said, openly appraising him. "You know, dark hallways, small rooms. You never know who might be lurking in the shadows."

"Somehow I suspect you're the real danger here," he said smoothly. "No red-blooded male would have a chance against two stunning women like you. Sandra, right?"

"Sadie," she corrected. "Nice to see you again, *Thomas*."

Tyler looked as if he wanted to say something, but then he burst into laughter. Linda stared at them both. Just like that, they were willing to forget about the deception? From the way Sadie was beaming at him, Linda knew what she was thinking. Husband material. Tyler was good-looking, he was charming and it didn't hurt the cause that he was the baby's father. Sadie could no more give up her campaign to get Linda married than she could resist doling out advice.

"Tyler, how about some coffee?" Sadie asked. "When a man calls a woman stunning, he deserves to be rewarded. But I have to warn you, my brew is the stuff legends are made of. Rumor has it, it could grow hair on a bowling ball."

"For heaven's sake, it's just decaf," Linda said curtly, pulling his jacket from the hall closet. She thrust it into his arms. "Besides, he didn't come for coffee. He came for this."

"Actually, I'd forgotten all about the jacket, but thanks." He took the garment and frowned. "I hate these things. Sports jackets, suits, ties…especially those penguin suits they make you wear at weddings. They make a man feel confined."

"Weddings or cummerbunds?" Sadie asked slyly.

The woman wouldn't give up. Linda shot her a warning glance.

Tyler laughed again. "I'd better watch what I say. I remember you telling me that you were engaged." He smiled at Linda. "But you're right. I didn't come for coffee. I came to take you out for breakfast. I figure since I said I'd take you to your car, why not make a full morning of it?"

His smile revealed the most adorable dimple in his right cheek. Why hadn't she noticed that before? Stop staring, she ordered herself. She tried to think of a snappy refusal, but nothing came to mind. Apparently, her newfound talent for quick retorts had suddenly vanished, taking her tongue with it.

"But you might want to put on some clothes before we go out," he said, looking at her with raised eyebrows.

With horror, she realized she was still in her bathrobe. Here she was, standing next to him, practically naked. Instinctively her hands went to the opening of her robe, and she tightened the sash around her waist. Okay, so maybe practically naked wasn't quite accurate.

The thick terry cloth robe covered most of her body, but still, what could he be thinking of her? What sort of woman answered the door wearing only a bathrobe?

And why oh why was her mind a blank? "Um…I can't go with you to breakfast. I've already eaten." So there, she thought absurdly.

Sadie waved her hand dismissively. "You call one measly piece of toast breakfast? Go on and get dressed. I'll keep your friend company." She put her arm through Tyler's. "Come on into the kitchen and I'll fix you that coffee."

There was no way Linda would leave Sadie alone with Tyler. Before Sadie was finished with him, she'd probably have him dressed as a penguin, waddling down the aisle.

Then again, maybe not. Tyler didn't seem like someone who let others make his decisions. Nevertheless, recalling the embarrassing things Sadie had once said to Frank, Linda wanted her friend out of the apartment. "A great cook…handy with a needle and thread…a talented decorator…" For someone who detested lying, Sadie did her share of embellishing the truth. Linda, a great cook? Sure, if cooking meant popping a carton into the microwave. Handy with a needle and thread meant she could replace a button. And decorating? Didn't she recently hang a Picasso print on her bedroom wall?

"Sadie, remember that sweatshirt you borrowed last week? I need it. Come with me while I get dressed."

"I don't remember borrow—"

"Now," Linda said emphatically. Ignoring Tyler's quizzical look, she bulldozed Sadie out of the living room.

Sadie plopped down on Linda's bed. "You're not seriously planning to wear a sweatshirt, are you? What kind of bait is that?" She studied Linda critically. "Why don't you put in your contact lenses? I can't understand why you bought them if you never intend to wear them."

"Shh!" Linda whispered furiously. "He might hear you! I only bought those stupid things to get you to stop nagging me after that fiasco at the hotel. Just because I didn't wear my glasses that night didn't mean I wanted to get rid of them. And never mind the sweatshirt. Don't you have somewhere to go?"

Sadie was wearing black tights under silver spandex shorts, her Run For Life T-shirt peeking out from under a maroon windbreaker. A fitness buff who ran three miles a day, she'd planned on jogging before driving Linda to the restaurant. "Okay, I can take a hint. I'm leaving. I take it this means my services are no longer required. I assume you're letting Tyler take you to your car?"

"Yes," Linda said, flustered. "I mean no. Oh, just go, all right?"

Sadie's eyes grew serious. "Are you sure, honey? I can stay, if you don't want to be alone with him. Just say the word. I'll do whatever you say."

"I'll be fine." The mischievous twinkle reappeared in Sadie's eyes, and Linda peered at her with suspicion. "What is it?"

"Well, since you asked… He's got that look all over him. I recognized it immediately. I saw it on Frank's face, just before he popped the question. Maybe Tyler isn't the scumbag I thought he was. Maybe he aims to do the right thing."

"Right for who? Him? You? I don't want what you

want, remember?" Apparently what they'd talked about last night hadn't sunk in. Linda sighed. She knew it wasn't her friend's fault. Sadie had been watching over her for so long, she didn't know how to stop. "Go for your jog. The sooner I deal with Tyler, the sooner all this will be behind me." Hadn't Sadie said that a person had to confront her demons before she could move on?

"Uh-huh." With a wink Sadie stood up, then left the room. "Catch you later!" Linda heard her say to Tyler, in a singsong voice.

The front door clicked shut and Linda let out a breath of relief. But her relief was short-lived. The task of dealing with Tyler still lay ahead. What if Sadie was right? What if he'd come here to propose? It wasn't as if marriage hadn't crossed his mind. "If I agreed to marry you," he'd said last night on the beach.

It's a conspiracy, she thought, pulling her denim skirt from her closet. The whole world was plotting to get her to the altar. She deliberated between a bulky wool sweater and an oversize pullover. Why were all her clothes so *big?* She considered borrowing something of Sadie's. That low-cut cashmere sweater would be a little tight across the chest, but so what? It would look great with the denim skirt. She was halfway out the door to Sadie's room, when she stopped in her tracks. What on earth was she doing? The idea was to send Tyler away, not lure him in, as Sadie had suggested. She chose the bulky sweater.

As she dressed, she tried to plan what she'd say to him. She had to make it clear that she wanted nothing from him. But the fact remained that he was the father.

What if he insisted on being in his child's life? Could she deny him? More importantly, could she deny her child? Both she and Tyler knew what it was like growing up without a father.

A wave of anxiety spilled through her. What if he sued for custody? What if that was the reason he wanted to test the baby's paternity? He could be planning to use the evidence in court.

Her head was spinning. Recalling Sara's words about remaining rational, she breathed in deeply, forcing herself to calm down. The idea of Tyler suing for custody was preposterous. What court would grant custody to a man who lived with constant danger?

She and Tyler would go out for breakfast and they would talk. Calmly. Rationally. She was sure they could reach an agreement, but if they failed, if he so much as hinted at custody, she'd fight him tooth and nail.

An image came to mind, and in spite of her anxiety she smiled. She pictured the two of them donning boxing gloves, prancing around each other in the ring. "Shake hands and come out fighting," she imagined the referee saying. Maybe she and Tyler would do it in reverse. Maybe they'd emerge from the ring as friends.

Why not? The more she thought about being friends, the more it made sense. If he insisted on being in his child's life, it would be easier on everyone if they weren't foes. She could handle friendship. Friendship between a man and a woman was perfectly acceptable.

She pulled the sweater off and tossed it onto the bed, choosing to wear a cream-colored jersey instead. It didn't plunge the way Sadie's cashmere sweater did, but it was soft and feminine. Her choice had nothing to do with his inviting smile or compelling eyes, she told herself. It had nothing to do with the way her skin had tingled under his gaze.

Tyler was studying the photographs on the mantel when she joined him in the living room. "Is she always like that?" he asked, glancing up.

In spite of her resolve to remain calm, she couldn't just stand there listening to someone put down her best friend. "Sadie means well," she said tightly. "She would go to the ends of the earth for me."

"No, I mean, does she always have that much energy? It tires me out just watching her. But I like her. She has spunk."

Oh. He was only trying to make conversation. No sense biting his head off just because she was terrible at small talk. "Sadie is Sadie. We make a good team. We balance each other. She's messy and disorganized, I'm a neatness freak. She's artistic, I'm practical. She's extroverted, I'm—" She stopped abruptly.

"Levelheaded," he filled in for her. "That was the first thing I thought about you when we met."

Levelheaded? That was supposed to be a compliment? That was what he'd found attractive about her? He was making fun of her, she decided. She'd been anything but levelheaded in that skimpy skirt and halter top, and now he was throwing her trampy behavior back in her face. "You don't have to be insulting," she said, bristling.

He put down the photos. "Just for one minute, can you stop thinking of me as the enemy? Let's pretend I'm just a guy and you're just a girl, and we're going out on a date. Simple. No complications. Do you think you can handle that?"

"I don't date."

He sighed. "Let me rephrase that. Think of us as two friends going out to share a meal, and since it was my idea, I'll treat."

She couldn't argue with his logic. Wasn't friendship the objective? "All right, but I insist on paying my own way."

"You're too late," he said. "I stopped at the market near my apartment and picked up a few things. We're dining alfresco. How does Douglas Park sound? It's just west of Douglas Street, right? Not too far from here."

Apparently, his idea of breakfast differed from hers. Who went on a picnic at eight o'clock in the morning? He'd parked his car just outside the building and, after stopping to collect what he'd bought, they set off for the park.

She peeked inside the bags in his arms as they strolled through the streets. "Looks like you thought of everything—cheeses, spreads, bagels, orange juice, even disposable picnic supplies. You haven't left anything out."

"No coffee, though. Not even decaf. It can't be good for the baby. I didn't want to drink it in front of you, knowing you shouldn't have any."

"That was considerate," she said with sincerity. Still, she was sure he was up to something. What if Sadie was right? What if he was planning to propose?

The park was surprisingly busy at this early hour. From the picnic area, she could see the basketball and tennis courts, which were quickly filling up. In the playground a few yards away, children were either playing in the sandbox or on swings, their voices resounding with delight.

An unfamiliar contentment took hold of her. Maybe there's something to be said for breakfast in the park, she thought. The sun was shining; the air was unseasonably warm. It was a beautiful, fogless San Francisco morning, a rare treat at this time of year. After they'd chosen a picnic table under a sweet-scented eucalyptus tree, Tyler put down the bags, and she began to empty them.

He was at her side immediately. "Here, let me do that."

"No, you carried these all the way here. The least I can do is set the table." She was conscious of his stare as she methodically folded the napkins in half, then in half again. "There now," she said, after inserting the plastic flatware into the pockets she'd created. She stood back and examined her work. "Isn't this nice?" Why was he looking at her like that? Just because this was a picnic didn't mean they had to be slobs. Besides, the sun was shining and it was a beautiful day. That alone was cause for celebration.

"Very elegant," he said, surprising her. "It's missing something, though." He picked up one of the bags and pulled out three red roses. "One for you, one for me and one for the baby," he explained, placing them into a large paper cup.

Her heart skipped a beat. Here it is, she thought. Here's where he's going to ask me to marry him. Here's where we're going to get into an argument.

He poured them each some juice. *"Santé,"* he said, raising his cup. "To your health."

She sighed with relief. Maybe Sadie was wrong. Maybe all Tyler wanted was to be friends. She felt herself relax. He had a comfortable way about him that made even small talk seem easy, and the next two hours seemed to pass in an instant. He made jokes; she laughed. And when she laughed, he smiled. They were both careful to avoid topics like their previous lives, exerting extra caution when it came to Walter. She talked about her job, though in generic terms, and about Sadie. He talked about his job in even more generic terms.

She lifted her face to the sunshine, basking in its warmth. She'd have to get out like this more often, she decided. Lately her stress level had risen at least a dozen notches. For one thing, the IRS was breathing down her neck—not that she or Walter had done anything wrong. She kept the books in impeccable order, and everything in them was on the up-and-up. But even more disturbing than being audited by the IRS was what was happening at work. On more than one occasion, people she could only describe as thugs had shown up unannounced, demanding to see Walter. No doubt they were trying to bully him into making illegal deals. Not that she was worried that he would comply. He wasn't that kind of man. But the whole thing had everyone at the office on edge.

Then, of course, there was the pregnancy. That alone had raised her stress level to record heights. Not to mention Sadie. In less than a week, she was getting married, leaving Linda to fend for herself.

Tyler began to clear the table. Interpreting this as a cue that their outing was over, her good mood suddenly vanished. What did you expect? she asked herself. He probably has a thousand things he'd rather do than spend an entire day with someone like me. She remembered Conrad's date from Sara's party. Weren't identical twins supposed to have the same preferences?

"Is this the sort of thing you usually do on a date?" she blurted. She felt her face redden. Now why had she gone and said that? She wasn't interested in him that way.

"I thought you said this wasn't a date," he said, a sly smile curling his lips.

She would have to learn to stop blushing. "I didn't mean to imply that it was. Dating hardly seems appropriate, given the situation."

He cocked his head. "All right then, if this isn't a date, what is it?"

"Two friends simply enjoying each other's company."

He looked amused. "Is that what we are? Friends?"

"Those were your words," she reminded him. "'Two friends going out to share a meal.' Given the situation—"

"You already said that."

This conversation was making her dizzy. "I already said what?"

"Situation. Why do you refer to the pregnancy as the situation?"

"Isn't that how you regard it?"

"No. A situation sounds like a problem. And it's not. I mean, yeah, it could be. But I have a solution."

She felt her chest constrict. Here it comes, she thought. Sadie was right, after all.

"I want you to marry me."

Bingo. I'll give him this much, Linda thought. He's bent on doing the right thing. But the problem was that, for him, the right thing seemed to change from moment to moment. "I wish I could promise you more than just now," he'd said that first night. "But it wouldn't be right."

Granted, his sudden turnabout was because of the baby. Babies did that. They had the power to change your perspective on a number of things. But not on the subject of husbands. The last thing she wanted in her life was a man telling her what to do.

She knew he was waiting for an answer. But what could she say without going into her past? Pensive, she looked over at the playground. A young mother was pushing a baby in a stroller, trying unsuccessfully to keep up with a boy of around three. "Johnny, you come back here this instant!" the woman yelled, but un-daunted, the boy darted ahead.

The mother looked frantic. The boy was headed straight for the swing set, where he'd surely be knocked down by either an empty chair let loose after someone had jumped, or by the legs of a child, kick-ing for momentum.

Apparently Tyler had also spotted the danger. He jumped to his feet and raced toward the playground. "Whoa there, tiger," he said as he swept the boy up, out of harm's way. He carried him back to his mother.

"Johnny, how many times have I warned you not to run ahead!" The woman took her son from Tyler's arms and held him tightly. "Thank goodness," she said into his hair. She shifted her son onto her hip and extended a hand to Tyler. "Hi, I'm Claudia Patterson. I can't thank you enough for your quick thinking. You are…?"

"Tyler Carlton," he answered. "Detective Carlton," he clarified, then smiled. "All in the line of duty, ma'am."

All in the line of duty, my foot, Linda thought, watching them. Couldn't he think of a better line? And why was that woman still holding his hand?

"A real live 'tectiv?" Johnny asked, his eyes wide. His face turned solemn. "Mommy, what's a 'tectiv?"

"He's a policeman," Claudia explained. "His job is to catch the bad guys and protect us." She gave Tyler a dazzling smile. "You can't possibly imagine how grateful I am."

Even from where Linda sat, she could tell that Claudia had more on her mind than gratitude. She deliberated what to do. She couldn't just sit there and not join them. That would be rude, wouldn't it? But she didn't want to suddenly appear at his side. That would be admitting she was jealous, which she most certainly was not.

"That's what I want to be, too!" Johnny exclaimed. "Can I be a 'tectiv when I'm all growed, Mommy?"

"I bet you're one of the fastest kids in the whole park," Tyler said, tousling his hair, "and in this business you have to be fast. There's just one thing," he added, pretending to be very serious. "You have to do a lot of looking around. That means looking where you're going. How else will you find the bad guys? And you have to be very, very careful. Like just now. You weren't very careful when you ran away from your mother. Do you know what I'm saying?"

The boy grinned. "Yeah. I better listen to my mom or else she won't take me to the park no more."

Tyler laughed. "I think he got the message," he said to the boy's mother. "He's one smart kid."

"Smart, but a handful. Never gives me a moment's rest. It's not easy raising two kids on your own. What about you?" she asked demurely. "You're good with children. Do you have any?"

Linda rolled her eyes. The woman was so obvious,

she could be neon. She wasn't asking if he had kids; she was asking if he had a wife.

"Not yet," he answered, motioning to Linda. "But I have one on the way."

Hearing his words, Linda felt a strange mix of smugness and relief. So there, you hussy, she thought, then realized she was being uncharitable. The woman was just trying to be friendly. And even if she had set her sights on Tyler, so what? It's not as if I care, Linda thought.

Pushing the stroller, the woman walked away, her son by her side. Linda waved at them. There was no reason she couldn't be gracious.

"Claudia was right," she said when Tyler had returned. "You're good with kids."

He sat down next to her at the table. "You sound surprised."

"Of course I'm surprised. I don't know you, Tyler. And that's why I can't marry you."

It was the truth. Even if she were inclined to get married, which she was not, how could she marry a man who was practically a stranger? Everything she knew about him was based on what she'd read in the papers and what she'd learned from his sister Sara. It was all hearsay. She couldn't take into account the night they'd spent at the hotel. They'd both pretended to be other people; all they'd learned about each other was bogus.

"Look at me, Linda." He cupped her chin with his hand. "Do you believe in fate? A wise man once said, 'God doesn't play dice.'"

"Wise is an understatement. Einstein was a genius. But I don't understand what—"

"Don't you see? We were meant to meet that night. The baby is proof. Every child comes into this world for a reason."

She stood up and began filling an empty paper bag with the trash from breakfast. "That might be true, but it has nothing to do with marriage. If every person is born for a reason, it follows that every child in this world has a right to be here. I believe that every baby is legitimate, which means we don't have to get married."

"We do if we want him to have a father."

She stopped what she was doing and looked down at him. "If you want to be a factor in his life, I won't stop you. You can see him as much as you want."

"I can't see him as much as I want unless I'm living with him. I want more for my child. I want what I never had." His tone took on a note of urgency. "I won't lie to you. It's more than that. When it comes to the subject of legitimacy, it's one thing to tell me what you believe, but it's another convincing the rest of the world. I want my kid to have my name."

"He will. I'll put it on the birth certificate." She wanted to assure him that everything would be all right, that their child would never feel the loneliness Tyler had suffered. She reached out to touch him, but shyness stopped her.

He crushed a paper cup with his fist and threw it onto the table. "That's not good enough. I want my child raised in a home with two parents. I'm not talking about common law, either. I want that piece of paper. What sort of role model would I be to my son if I didn't marry his mother? I want to be there for him, physically, morally and legally." His eyes darkened, and he seemed to disappear somewhere deep inside. "I know my mother did the best she could, but I also know that something was missing. It was as if her heart had been ripped from her body. Sara, Kathleen, Conrad…we all felt it, and we all suffered because of it. Walter was responsible, and I swear, if it takes me the rest of my life, I'll make him pay."

Linda recoiled, frightened by his anger. He wasn't just determined; he was obsessed. Suddenly, she felt foolish. What did she think he would do? He wasn't one of those thugs she'd seen at the office; he was a cop.

She regarded him closely, and saw the vulnerability in his eyes. In spite of her shyness, she touched the side of his face. "We don't even know each other," she said softly. "How can we get married?"

Either her touch or her tone must have mollified him, because all at once his anger dissolved. He took her hand and eased her back onto the bench.

His expression stilled. "I can wait, if I have to, but I think you're wrong. All we need to know we learned that night at the hotel. We haven't changed. We're still the same people we were two months ago."

She stared at him incredulously. "How can you say that? You're not Thomas and I'm not Lyla. We're not the same people at all."

"Granted, I lied about who I was, but only because I wanted to remain anonymous for as long as possible. In my line of work, some things are better kept secret, at least until we know who and what we're dealing with. San Francisco isn't such a big place. Your turning out to be Lyla is proof of that."

"But we were each just playing a role," she protested. She knew she was talking more about herself than she was about him, but the fact remained that they weren't who they'd claimed to be.

"You're still the same beautiful, shy but gutsy woman I made love to. Lyla or Linda, a name is just a tag. It doesn't change who you really are. We were drawn together then, just as we are now. You can't deny that there's something between us."

Gutsy? *Beautiful?* Who was he talking about? "There's nothing between us," she insisted. But even to her own ears, her protest sounded weak.

He broke into a wicked grin. "Are you sure?" He lowered his head, and her pulse went haywire. He was going to kiss her, and she felt powerless to resist.

Then, just like that, he withdrew. She looked up at him, unsure if she felt hurt or relieved. What had just happened? Had she done something wrong?

"I don't want you to do anything you don't want to," he said soberly. "I'm not happy, but I'm willing to wait as long it takes."

Her confusion deepened. Was he talking about marriage or sex? But how could he mean sex, when they'd already made love? Unless, she reasoned, he'd finally accepted that they'd been two different people that night. In a sense, the next time would be their first time.

Not that there'd be a next time, she reminded herself.

Nevertheless, she was moved. If he was willing to wait—for sex or for marriage—he believed she was worth waiting for. She heard her mother's voice in her head, warning her not to trust him. She forced the voice away.

Sitting so close to him on the bench, she felt a vaguely sensuous quivering. His thigh grazed hers, sending an unwanted fluttering coursing through her body. She didn't want to feel this, didn't want to feel anything for him. Yet in spite of her reserve, she lifted her head to his, as though an invisible force was directing her. And still he held back. She parted her lips. He didn't flinch. She brought her hand behind his neck and slowly lowered his head to hers. His lips brushed alongside her cheek, sending an electric shock ricocheting down her spine.

"Linda," he murmured, speaking her name tentatively as if, sensing her reluctance, he was asking if she was sure. She wasn't sure of anything. All she was aware of was the heady scent of his aftershave and the feel of his lips on her skin as his breath mingled with hers.

He must have taken her silence as acquiescence, because he placed his hands around the small of her back, turning her to him, drawing her even closer. She melted into him easily, as though in his arms she knew she was safe. In his arms, she was protected.

And then it happened.

She stiffened.

Then she pulled away.

"Linda…"

"No, don't say it."

His voice was so soft she had to strain to hear. "Linda, what are you afraid of?"

She lowered her eyes. Then, with an honesty that surprised her, she looked up and met his gaze. "Everything," she whispered.

Chapter Five

He thought his heart would dissolve.

He wanted to take her back into his arms and hold her tightly but, believing he would only frighten her more, he resisted the urge.

"I would never hurt you," he said softly.

"You don't understand. There are things about me you don't know. Things in my past." She stared straight ahead, gazing toward the playground. "And that's where I want them to remain."

"Linda, look at me," he prodded gently. "You don't have to keep everything bottled inside. Talk to me. Let me help."

She let out a small laugh. "You're saying I should trust you. Now that's almost funny, coming from you."

He winced. "I wish we could turn back the clock and start over, but we can't. We have to move forward. We have another life to consider. We have our baby. If it were just about us, we could forget about that night and go our separate ways, but it's not."

Could he? he wondered. If she weren't pregnant, could he just walk away?

She sighed. "Sorry. I didn't mean to snap at you. It's just that trust isn't something I do easily. I don't feel…safe." Her voice took on a hard edge. "My mother was murdered. There, I said it. Are you satisfied?"

He knew he should appear shocked, but in truth, he already knew about her mother. He'd read about the murder in Robert Jackson's report, back in July.

He also knew how difficult it must have been for Linda to say the words aloud. The least he could do was match her honesty. "I know," he said.

He pictured the photos attached to the file. That night in the lounge of the hotel, he'd thought that Linda looked familiar, but he'd attributed the familiarity to his fantasies. "You're the woman of my dreams," he'd told her after they'd made love. Last night, he would have cringed at the memory of the words, but this morning… Hell, he didn't know how he felt.

Sitting next to her at the picnic table, he braced himself for the attack. Even though he'd read the report before he'd met her, he was sure she would accuse him of spying.

"Yes, I suppose you do know," she said, surprising him. "It's your job." When she spoke again, her voice sounded hollow, as though coming from a distance. "I was seventeen. I was out with…friends. When I got home, there were police cars everywhere. Someone had broken into the house. A robbery, they called it. As if we had anything worth stealing. His name was Timothy Sands, and he was much older than the other boys, but I guess you know that, too."

"You went to live with your sister," Tyler filled in. "When she and her husband were killed in a car crash, you left Montana to live with Sadie." No one should have to go through so much, he thought, a lump forming in his throat. He wanted to promise he'd never let anything happen to her again, but he refrained. He knew it was a promise he might not be able to keep. No one could.

Her expression was contrite. "I'd told you I was from Wisconsin. I've never even been there."

"Lyla from Wisconsin," he said, smiling sadly.

"You probably also know that I testified against Timothy at the trial, and that my testimony helped to convict him. I knew him from school. He hung around with…a friend of mine."

She didn't continue, and Tyler searched his memory. According to the file, she'd confided to someone— David Farber, he recalled, or was it Daniel?—about her mother's jewelry. Farber, in turn, had tipped off Sands. Tyler looked at Linda with confusion. Something didn't jibe. Only a moment ago, she'd told him that she and her mother hadn't owned anything worth stealing.

"Timothy was given a life sentence with no possibility of parole," she continued, her voice still sounding far away. "I thought that was the end of it, but four years ago, he was released on a technicality. I was terrified he'd come after me. There were phone calls…threats…" She took a moment to compose herself. "Walter hired someone to dig into Timothy's past. As a result, Timothy was tried and convicted for a similar crime. To this day, I'm convinced that Walter saved my life. But I guess you know that, too."

He tried to hide his surprise. He'd known about the second trial, but not about Walter's involvement. He now understood the reason for her unwavering loyalty. Gratitude went a long way. But it was more than just gratitude that tied her to Walter; it was blind devotion. How could the man who had helped put away her mother's murderer do any wrong?

Tyler suspected there was more to the story than what she'd told him. Certainly more than what was in the report. But he knew she'd never trust him with the truth as long as she held on to her delusions about Walter. How could she trust him when he was so intent on destroying the one man she believed in? He had to prove to her that he wasn't the bad guy in the story. It wouldn't be easy. She'd never believe anything he'd say against Walter.

But she might believe someone else. Someone officially assigned to the case.

He rose from the picnic table and took her hand. "Come on, let's go. I want to make a stop before I take you to your car. There's someone I want you to meet."

"Are you sure I can't get you anything?" Brooke asked. Tyler's cousin set the coffeepot onto the table.

"We ate at the park," Linda said, "but thank you." She gazed around the café. Through the glass door of the refrigerator she could see an assortment of cakes and pastries; on the shelf next to the espresso machine was a variety of teas. A half-dozen tables crowded the little bistro, giving it a European flavor. Right now, however, the other five tables were empty. She turned to Brooke, who had sat down next to her husband, Mark. "I'm surprised you're open on Sunday."

"We're open seven days a week," Brooke said with pride.

"We stay open on Sundays because of the competition," Mark offered, putting his arm around Brooke's shoulders. "This café is a recent addition. In another hour, the place will be crowded. No rest for the wicked, I always say. Brooke just about lives here."

Brooke waved at him dismissively. "Oh, don't listen to him. I don't work every day. I do like to come in on the weekend, though. It's our busiest time, and I enjoy talking to the customers. It also allows me to give the staff more time off. Dad will be here later, too." She smiled affectionately at her husband. "Mark comes in to help, whenever he's not out and about chasing criminals."

"The greatest drawback to marriage," Mark said, "is that sleeping late on your day off becomes a thing of the past."

Brooke playfully poked him in the ribs. "I didn't hear you complaining when I nudged you at six."

Linda glanced at her and then back at Mark. It took her a moment before she realized that they were teasing each other. It took her another moment before she realized what Brooke had meant. Good heavens, was everyone in this family so casual about sex?

Tyler laughed. "Wait till you have kids. I'm told this will seem like a holiday."

"What about you, Ty?" Mark asked, and Linda nearly choked. "What brings you here so early? Granted, it's nearly eleven, but it's still morning. Don't you always sleep until noon on your day off?"

Now that's a surprise, Linda thought. He'd shown up at her apartment at eight, hadn't he? But then she remembered the morning at the hotel. When she'd slipped out of bed, he hadn't even stirred.

"I wanted Linda to meet you," he said. "We left the party before she had a chance."

Brooke nodded. "Yes, we know. I'm glad you're feeling better, Linda. You gave us quite a scare."

A silence fell over the group. What? Linda thought. She looked at Mark and then back at Brooke. Did they know? But how? It couldn't have come from Sadie. Which left Sara. Good grief, if Sara was telling everyone who was family, the whole city would be buzzing with the news.

"Word travels fast," Brooke said, as though Linda had spoken out loud. "Mark's brother Nick was here earlier this morning." She smiled warmly. "Now that all this is out in the open, I'm sure we're going to be seeing a lot of you."

Nick? Wasn't he Tyler's partner? Linda shot Tyler a poisonous look. Apparently he'd been busy since he left her last night. He was the one who had spilled the beans, not Sara. Who else had he told?

Mark winked at Linda. "It sure took this guy long enough to find you. Nick told us that Tyler combed every bar in the city."

Tyler had looked for her? Now this was news. But she was more relieved than surprised. They weren't talking about the baby; they were talking about the night at the hotel. Her relief quickly vanished, and she felt herself blushing. She peered at Tyler. What exactly had he told his partner?

Tyler shifted in his chair. "Mark…" he warned.

But his friend was relentless. "You should have put me on the trail, Ty," he said, half joking, half serious. "It would have saved you a lot of time."

Linda's ears perked up. "Are you on the police force, too?"

"Nope, I'm strictly private."

"A private investigator?"

Mark laughed. "Yeah, but Tyler went after you all on his own. We wouldn't have even known about Lyla if Nick hadn't spilled the beans."

At the park, when Tyler had talked about his cousin, Brooke, he'd also mentioned his partner, Nick. He'd told her that Nick had an older brother, Mark, but she hadn't realized that this was the same Mark she'd read about in the newspapers. Mark Banning. The man who caught the gunman who'd tried to kill Brooke's father. The gunman, the papers had speculated, whom Walter had hired.

"Mark!" Brooke reprimanded. "Can't you see you're embarrassing them?"

"Remind me to speak to Nick," Tyler grumbled.

"Now don't be too hard on him," Brooke said. "It was my fault. You've been acting weird these past two months, and after you disappeared with Linda last night, I thought there might be a connection. When Nick came by for coffee this morning, I pried it out of him."

Tyler shrugged. "Water under the bridge."

"All's well that ends well," she said, brightening.

Mark chuckled. "When it comes to matters of the heart, my wife thinks she's Dear Miss Lonelyhearts. If it were up to her, everyone would be in a relationship."

Brooke rolled her eyes, but it was obvious she wasn't offended. "It seems to have done you a world of good," she pointed out.

"Yes, dear," Mark said, and the two of them laughed. He took his wife's hand, and she gave him an adoring look.

"Life sure plays funny tricks," Tyler said out of the blue. "If it hadn't been for the investigation, you and Brooke wouldn't be together now."

Mark shot him a warning glance. Tyler nodded, ever so slightly, and Mark seemed to relax in his chair.

An alarm went off in Linda's head. What was that about?

"Have you come up with anything new on the Parks case?" Tyler asked casually.

Too casually, as far as Linda was concerned. Why would he even ask that? If something had broken in the case, wouldn't he already be on top of it? Besides, she didn't know much about police procedure, but she didn't think they should be discussing the case in front of her. Wasn't he breaking some sort of code, like the Hippocratic oath?

"Off the record, of course," he qualified, as though privy to her thoughts.

"I'm not breaking any confidentiality when I say this," Mark said in a contrived-sounding voice. "Walter and his empire are in for a fall. The D.A. is close to pressing charges, and there's no doubt in my mind that he'll get a conviction." He turned to Linda. "You'll probably be subpoenaed, but there's no reason for you to worry. We know your hands are clean. But if there's anything you want to come forward with, now would be the time."

What was that supposed to mean? Was Mark imply-ing that she could be accused of withholding evidence? She regarded him through narrowed eyes. She felt as if she were a suspect in a second-rate cop show. Tyler and Mark were playing good cop, bad cop, except she didn't know who was supposed to be who. One thing she was certain of, however. This meeting was a setup to get her to talk. Well, it wasn't working. Even if she were in-clined to help them, which was unthinkable, what could she possibly say? Walter hadn't done anything wrong.

She sat back in her chair, anger stirring inside her. It was apparent why Tyler had brought her here. He thought he could scare her into defecting to his side.

Brooke jumped to her feet. "No shop talk on Sun-day," she said, as though sensing Linda's discomfort. "Come on, Linda. Let me show you around the book-store before it gets crowded. Do you like browsing through rare books? We just got in an entire case of first editions."

Glad to put an end to Tyler's obvious charade, Linda followed Brooke into the adjoining bookstore, and the next hour passed quickly and pleasurably. The two women perused unusual books while the men, Linda as-sumed, discussed the case.

Unless they were discussing *her*.

"I have something extraordinary to show you," Brooke said with pride. "I'll be right back."

Linda picked up a book of Emily Dickinson's poems and let her mind wander. She recalled the conversation in the café, particularly Mark's comment about Tyler combing the city, looking for her. If what he'd said was true, then Tyler hadn't known who she was at the hotel, after all. Which meant he hadn't sought her out specifically to obtain information.

She wasn't sure if Mark was totally on the up-and-up, but she'd warmed to Brooke immediately, finding no reason to distrust her, and Brooke had confirmed what Mark had said.

Linda was torn with conflicting emotions. Maybe she'd judged Tyler too quickly. Maybe he hadn't brought her here to scare her into talking. What if, knowing she'd never believe anything he'd say regarding Walter, he'd simply wanted to warn her that her life was about to undergo changes?

Changes she'd need to prepare for, changes that had nothing to do with the baby.

Although she didn't want to believe what Mark had said about the case, what if it were true? What if Walter was convicted? For the first time since this nasty business began, she had doubts. Not about Walter's innocence—of that, she was certain—but about the future. She wasn't just thinking about herself; she was worried about the baby. How would they live? She'd be the ex-accountant of a convicted embezzler. Fat chance of her finding work again in this city. As Tyler had said, San Francisco wasn't such a big place.

She forced herself to focus on more cheerful thoughts. She recalled how Tyler had related to the boy in the park, and a smile came to her lips. The boy's mother had been right when she'd said he had a way with kids.

Ah, yes, Claudia. It would also seem that Tyler wasn't the philanderer his twin brother was, or he would have been more receptive to the woman's obvious offer.

It was ironic, Linda thought. Here she was, terrified of guns, and she was seriously considering marrying a man who carried one.

She set down the book she'd been leafing through. Wait a minute. Seriously considering?

Well, why not? Even if Walter wasn't convicted, her future was uncertain. Where would she live if she had to give up her apartment? How could she raise the baby by herself? Not only that, she was terrified at the prospect of living alone. Tyler was a cop, which meant he could provide her with the protection she desperately craved.

Whether she liked it or not, seriously considering was what she was doing.

For some reason the expression, "Keep your friends close and your enemies closer," popped into her head. She dismissed it immediately. Tyler wasn't her enemy. He wanted to marry her, didn't he?

She wouldn't kid herself into thinking his proposal had to do with anything other than the baby and, to be honest, she preferred it that way. If he didn't expect more from her, he wouldn't be disappointed. But if she accepted his proposal—and that was a big if—it didn't mean she'd cross over to his side of the case. The marriage and Walter would have to remain two separate matters.

Of course, anything she might just happen to learn as Tyler's fiancée would be an added bonus. A disturbing thought occurred to her. He could very well be thinking along those same lines.

Smiling, Brooke returned with a book in her hand. "Look at this," she said excitedly. "A first edition of

Jane Eyre. This is one of my favorite novels. It's got everything—love, marriage, suspense and drama."

Linda knew the story well. Don't forget deceit, she thought.

Tyler hadn't missed the look on Linda's face when he'd brought up the case. How could he have been so naive? Had he really believed that talking to Mark would get her to see the truth?

This is what happens when you let a woman under your skin, he thought. It clouds your judgment.

"I like your cousin," she said as they drove to the restaurant to pick up her car. "She's a down-to-earth, genuinely caring person. She went out of her way to make me feel at home."

Was he hearing right? Linda had been as wired as a surveillance van. He gave her a quick glance. She was smiling brightly. Okay, so maybe she meant what she'd said. He couldn't deny that she and Brooke had clicked like old friends.

He had to loosen up. This whole business was turning him into a cynic. "She liked you, too. I imagine we'll be seeing a lot more of her and Mark." He let out a chuckle.

"What's so funny?"

"It's just that everywhere I turn, more relatives crop up. My Christmas list keeps growing and growing."

"But you must have known that your mother had a younger brother," she pointed out.

"Yes, but Derek—Brooke's father—disappeared before I was born. I only recently found out that I had a cousin. Mark, by the way, was instrumental in locating my uncle."

Tyler glanced at her again, but this time her face was blank. He tried to figure out what she was thinking. From her reaction earlier in the café, he'd assumed she hadn't known about Mark's role in the investigation. But how could she not have known? The newspapers had blown the P.I.'s cover to pieces. After Brooke had taken the bullet meant for Derek, the media had had a field day.

"It's a small world," Linda said. "It seems that lately everyone I meet is in some way connected to the Parks family."

"The Parks network, you mean." The Parks web, he thought grimly. We're the flies, and Walter is the spider.

"It's certainly complicated," she said evasively.

Did she know more than she was letting on? Hoping to draw her out, he proceeded with caution. "It can't be easy for Walter's children, not knowing what side of the fence to sit on." He was referring to Walter's legitimate children, not to him and Conrad. For him and his brother, the choice was clear.

"Yes, I imagine it would be. Though, of course, I wouldn't know. Some people might think that family problems are actually a blessing."

Now that was a strange comment, he thought. But then he recalled the photos on the mantle in her apartment. He'd figured they all belonged to Sadie, since Linda wasn't in any of them. Maybe the remark wasn't that strange, after all. Having family problems meant having a family. "This baby means a great deal to you," he said quietly.

She didn't answer right away. "Why didn't you tell them?"

"Tell who what?"

"Brooke and Mark. Nick. All of them. Why didn't you tell them I was pregnant?"

"Did you want me to?"

"I don't know. I guess it doesn't matter. They'll find out soon enough."

"I think we should wait until we decide what we're going to do." He wanted to say, "Until we decide on a wedding date," but he held back.

"All right," she said.

His heart jumped. "All right, what?"

"Blood test, DNA test, whatever. I don't know much about these things. I'll do whatever you want. You have a right to be sure."

Was this her way of accepting a proposal? "Linda, I don't want to have the baby tested. I know it's mine."

"But you said—"

"I know what I said, and I was wrong." He pulled into the parking lot of the restaurant and turned off the ignition. "Linda, hear me out. In the instant I first laid eyes on you, my whole world turned upside down. Call it fate, if you want. Or destiny. I know it sounds crazy, but these days nothing seems to make much sense. Yet there are two things I'm sure of. One, the baby is mine. Two, we should get married."

"Fate," she repeated flatly. "That's what Brooke said. She and Mark met in August, and now they're married. She said that sometimes it happens that way. Sometimes you know right from the start, even though you might not admit it."

He'd known right away, too, the first time he'd seen Linda, but if anyone had told him he could feel like that, he would have laughed. "Sounds like you and Brooke had an interesting conversation."

"But I'm not convinced," she continued. "I still think a couple needs to spend time together before making a commitment."

So it was back to that. So much for thinking she wanted to marry him. Well, if dating was what she wanted, dating was what she'd get. Except it had better be the condensed version. He wanted to get married before their child was born.

She unfastened her seat belt and reached for the door. "Um, I had a nice time. Thank you for breakfast."

He had to suppress a smile. She sounded like a schoolgirl. "Can I see you later? What about dinner?" he asked, not bothering to hide his eagerness. With amusement, he realized that he probably sounded as young as she did.

She hesitated. "I promised Sadie I'd help her pack."

"What about tomorrow? I can pick you up at noon, and we can go to lunch."

She looked horrified. "Come to the office? I don't think so. The atmosphere at work is tense enough."

She had a point. Meeting her at the office wasn't such a good idea, now that the DNA had hit the fan. "All right, meet me somewhere. Let's have dinner later, too. I want to spend time with you."

She gave him an apologetic smile. "I'm going to be tied up all this week helping Sadie. We have a ton of last-minute details to take care of, and then there's the rehearsal, not to mention the dinner for the out-of-town guests."

He shook his head. Dating had never seemed so difficult. "When is it?"

"The rehearsal dinner's on Friday. But—"

"No, I mean the wedding."

She peered at him with suspicion. "Saturday. Why?"

"What time?"

"The ceremony is at five, but the photographer arrives at four. Why?" she repeated.

"I'll pick you up at your apartment at three." He smiled at her slyly. "Unless, of course, you already have a date." Somehow he knew she didn't.

"No, but—"

"Then it's settled. I'll see you on Saturday."

Maybe, just maybe, seeing her best friend get married would trigger a response. Weddings were supposed to be contagious, weren't they? If so, he'd be right there beside her when she succumbed.

"Say cheese!"

Linda sat next to Tyler at the head table, watching couples whirl around the dance floor. A flash exploded in her face as the photographer snapped their picture. The guests at the other tables tinkled their glasses with their spoons, a sign for the bride and groom to kiss. The photographer focused his camera on the happy couple, who didn't disappoint the guests.

Linda thought back over the past week. It had been long and arduous with last-minute preparations and one catastrophe after another. Two members of the band had come down with chicken pox, and Sadie and Linda had had to scramble for another group. The tablecloths and napkins were not what Sadie had ordered, but after the caterer agreed to knock down the price, Sadie decided that pale yellow went well with her dusty-rose scheme after all. In the end, the whole affair was proceeding without a hitch.

The evening had begun at St. Francis Church and was now winding down at Windsor Hall, where the reception was being held. Overlooking the Bay, the banquet room was ornately decorated with flowers in a tradition of warmth and elegance. A silver candelabra glistened at each end of the head table, the other tables adorned with candled centerpieces. On the small stage a three-piece band played an eclectic mix of dance music as couples moved across the floor in the muted lighting.

Linda was filled with happiness for her friend. But something else filled her, as well, something unfamiliar, as she watched the blissful couple raise champagne glasses to each other's lips. It was unfamiliar because she'd never before felt this strange mixture of envy and poignancy.

"Care to dance?" Tyler asked, strikingly handsome in a formal suit and tie.

She imagined herself in his arms, moving to the rhythm, floating across the dance floor…stepping on his toes. "Uh, I don't think so," she mumbled, ashamed to admit she didn't know how.

Refusing to take no for an answer, he took her hand and eased her from her chair. The music was playing something foreign, and she looked up at him with doubt. "I don't know about this, Tyler. Why don't we get some punch instead?" She gestured to a table where frozen baby roses bobbed in a large crystal bowl.

"I don't trust anything that's been spiked with flowers," he joked, leading her to the dance floor. "Don't worry, it's easy. Before this dance is over, you'll be a real *milonguera*."

She looked at him warily. "A real what?"

He gently extended her arm. Clasping her hand, they moved across the floor in a rhythmic stroll. "A *milonguera* is a woman whose life revolves around the tango," he explained. "ONE, two, THREE, four. That's it. You're getting it. It's easy when you allow yourself to feel the beat. Slow and steady. Step when I do, only on the major beats."

Good grief, the tango? What next? Skydiving? One thing about Tyler, he was a man of surprises. "Where did you learn this?"

"Pay attention, Linda. Look to the right. Keep the weight over the balls of your feet, but don't stand on your toes—it'll tire you out. ONE, two, THREE, four. ONE, two, THREE, four. By the way, dancing isn't my only talent. There's a lot about me you don't know, and I intend to spend the rest of my life showing you."

Suddenly, he pivoted around and faced the other way. To her amazement she ended up in the same direction, moving gracefully along the ballroom floor. He was right. It was easy once you let yourself feel the music. She closed her eyes, imagining she was a jungle cat, slinky and beautiful.

He placed his arms around her waist, lowering her into a dip. She opened her eyes, and their gazes locked. A rainbow of butterflies fluttered in her stomach. Maybe it was the sexy tempo of the music, or maybe it was the way he was looking at her, but she knew that this time if he tried to kiss her, right there on the dance floor, she wouldn't pull away.

The music came to a halt, and he whirled her up to her feet. "Not bad for a beginner," he said, casting her a devilish grin.

She wanted to make a clever retort, but as usual, nothing came to mind. The music started up again, and he pulled her back into his arms. Saved by the bell, she thought. Or in this case, by the band.

The tempo of the music was leisurely, and Tyler pulled her closer. At least slow dancing doesn't require any special skill, she thought.

Saved by the band? Hardly. Locked in Tyler's embrace, she was acutely aware of the danger as they slowly swayed to the music, hardly moving at all. She felt his breath on her neck, his cheek grazing hers.

"Have I told you how lovely you look tonight?" he murmured in her ear.

Usually, she detested being part of a wedding party, not because she was forced to wear an outfit that inevitably made her feel like an ostrich, but because she didn't like the attention as she walked down the aisle. But tonight, as Sadie's maid of honor, she'd felt as if she'd been floating on air. A princess out for a stroll.

She'd balked when Sadie had chosen this design. Far from traditional, the satin gown plunged in the front and was practically backless. Okay, so it wasn't hideous. In fact, it was stunning. And seductive. But neither stunning nor seductive was exactly her style.

Suddenly the music stopped, and the lights brightened. "And now, ladies," the band leader announced, "the bride is going to throw the bouquet. We need all the single ladies out here. Come on down, don't be shy!"

Tyler practically threw her into the crowd.

She retreated to the back of the room.

"Are you ready, Sadie?" the musician spoke into the microphone. "Here we go. On the count of three…"

From the stage up front, Sadie caught her eye. Don't, Linda silently begged. Don't you dare.

"…three!"

But, of course, Sadie couldn't hear her, and even if she could, Linda knew it wouldn't make a difference. With a determined look her friend hurled the bouquet straight at Linda. It soared through the air, clear across the room. If Sadie's business ever failed, Linda thought, she could always become a quarterback for the 49ers.

Alone at the back of the room, she felt as if everyone was watching her. Watching and waiting, cheering her on. She froze. What to do? What to do? She couldn't just stand there and deliberately drop the darn thing.

Oh, what the heck. Why not go for it? It was just a dumb custom. Didn't mean a thing. She braced herself, extended her arms—here it comes!

Heidi, Sadie's seven-year-old niece, had made a mad dash down the sidelines, and before anyone could bat an eye ran right out in front of Linda. What to do? What to do? Heidi looked so adorable in her flower girl's dress; how could Linda disappoint her? Linda deliberately fumbled, and Heidi made the catch. The watching guests laughed and applauded.

Tyler returned to Linda's side, looking annoyed. "What's your problem?"

"Excuse me?" Standing on display at the back of the room had made her feel uncomfortable; she didn't need his attitude, as well.

The band broke into a lively polka. "Let's get out of here," Tyler said, raising his voice to be heard over the oompah-pahs coming from the stage. His hand on her elbow, he guided her out into the lobby, where it was quieter.

"I can't believe you're angry over a bunch of flowers."

He sighed. "It's not about the stupid flowers. It's about us. You. Me. The baby. I want to get married as soon as possible."

"What happened to your not pressuring me?" she asked, pulling her arm free. "Just a few days ago, you said you were willing to wait as long as it took. Now suddenly, you're singing a different tune. How am I supposed to trust you when you keeping changing your mind?"

"I haven't changed my mind about marriage. But I want to be a father to this child before he comes into the world."

She took a deep breath. "Well, then fine."

"Well, then fine, what? Why do I feel like I'm on a merry-go-round? Could you be a little more specific?"

"Well, then fine, I'll marry you."

He looked stunned, as if he couldn't figure out what had just happened. "Just like that you change *your* mind?"

She planted her hands on her hips. "Look, do you want to marry me or not?"

He leaned in close, and she dropped her arms. She studied his face. Was he going to kiss her? She couldn't be sure. She'd thought he was going to kiss her when he'd dipped her on the dance floor, but she'd been wrong.

The butterflies in her stomach returned, this time

with a vengeance. Go away, she implored. I don't want to feel this. Butterflies or not, she couldn't let her libido interfere with real life. She knew all too well what happened when you gave in to the fluttering.

He touched her cheek, his fingers against her skin sending shivers down her spine. "The last thing I want is to make love to a woman who isn't interested," he said quietly. "But eventually I want us to have a real marriage. You can deny it all you want, but there's something between us. I felt it that night at the hotel, and it's still there."

She stepped out of his reach. "I won't lie to you, Tyler. I said I'd marry you, but there's a condition. This has to be a marriage of convenience, or the whole thing is off."

He didn't speak for a long moment, as though thinking over what she was implying. Then he nodded and said quietly, "If I have to live this way, I will. I intend to be a father to my child, and that means under any condition. But I won't lie to you, either. I'm not pleased with the arrangement."

He might not be pleased, but for her the setup was ideal. She would have safety, financial security and her child. She thought of it as a career move.

This job, however, wouldn't include fringe benefits.

Chapter Six

"I still don't understand why we have to get married here."

Linda sat next to Tyler on the gray tweed couch in the minister's office. In the corner of the room, a tall Queen Anne clock ticked away the seconds, competing with the pounding in her chest. If just meeting the minister made her so anxious, what would the actual ceremony do?

The wedding was turning into a nightmare. For the past five days since she'd accepted Tyler's proposal, they'd been arguing about the details. Not only did he want a church ceremony, he wanted his family and friends to witness the event. She could just imagine herself in a chaste wedding gown, walking down the aisle while scrutinizing eyes burned into her, making her feel like an insect in a jar. He also wanted to hold a reception at a fancy restaurant or hall, which she insisted wasn't going to happen.

"I already told you, this is where all the Carlton and Parks weddings take place," he said with impatience. "I intend to assume my place in the family, once and for all."

"I don't want to turn the wedding into a circus. If you invite your whole family, half of San Francisco will show up."

"I can't not ask my family to come," he protested. "And what about Sadie? Don't you want your best friend to be your matron of honor?"

"Let me remind you, our marriage is just an arrangement. Think of it as a business deal. You wouldn't invite your family or friends to a merger, would you? In any case, you said you want to get married as soon as possible, and as soon as possible doesn't leave room for much planning. Do you have any idea how long it took to put Sadie's wedding together?"

She could tell she wasn't getting anywhere with her reasoning, but then she had a stroke of genius. "If you want family at the ceremony, we'll have to invite Walter. If you're so insistent on having a traditional wedding, who else do I have who can give me away?" That was a bluff. How could she ask Walter to walk down the aisle when she didn't have the courage to tell him she was marrying his son?

Apparently the bluff worked, because Tyler caved in. At least on that point. "Fine," he said with resignation. "We'll have a small wedding. But I still want us to get married in this church."

"Churches are for *real* weddings," she said, attempting one last stab as they waited for the minister.

But Tyler was adamant. "Walter took everything, and it's high time I reclaimed what's rightfully mine. I'm not talking about money, I'm talking about a sense of belonging. Getting married in this church is just one step toward that, but it's a step in the right direction. No one will ever force me to be an outsider again."

She could see there was no dissuading him. Like everything else, this was about Walter. Scowling, she stared straight ahead.

"Tyler Carlton?" A sprightly-looking older man had entered the office and was smiling jovially. "I'm sorry to have kept you waiting. I couldn't find my appointment book. I'm Reverend Bob Nelson, and you," he said, nodding at Linda, "must be the bride." He sat down in the armchair across from the couch. "Oh dear, now where are my glasses?" Chuckling, he pulled them down from the top of his head. "Ah, right where I left them."

Bright assessing eyes peered at her from behind his wire-framed glasses. He looks more like a mad scientist than a man of the church, Linda thought, regarding his bushy white hair with uncertainty.

He opened the book on his lap, his face alight with merriment. "Wedding dates are usually set well in advance. If parents want to get the date they want, they should probably book the wedding as soon as their children are born. Of course, these days more and more young couples insist on planning their own weddings. On the one hand, I like to encourage their independent spirit, but on the other hand, it's always sad when a tradition is lost. How does a July wedding sound? We still have a Sunday open."

Linda's mood sank even lower. If July was the earliest date available, they'd have ample time to plan the kind of wedding Tyler wanted. If just the thought of getting married in front of an audience made her want to dig a hole and go into hiding, what would she feel like pushing a stroller down the aisle?

Tyler cleared his throat. "Reverend, I think you misunderstood me on the phone. We need to get married as soon as possible."

"I see," the minister said.

He knows, Linda thought, her face flaming. Could Tyler possibly have been any less subtle?

"All right, then," the minister said, pushing his glasses up on his nose. "Let's take another look." He studied the ledger. "The earliest date I can give you is in two weeks, if you don't mind getting married on a weekday."

"Two weeks!" Linda blurted. She didn't want to wait until July, but two weeks was way too soon. Growing accustomed to the idea that she was going to have a baby was easy; acquiring a husband was another matter. "That doesn't give us much time to get to know each other." She groaned inwardly. How could she have said something so stupid?

Tyler regarded her with impatience. "Linda, we've already been over this. As soon as possible doesn't mean sometime in the distant future."

The minister raised an eyebrow. "Just how long have you known each other?"

"We met a week before last Saturday," Linda answered nervously.

"I see," the minister said again. "Tyler, you don't have a problem with that?"

Tyler looked at him blankly, and then understanding registered in his face. "The baby is mine," he said tightly. "What my fiancée means is that we just found out who we are. We actually met in August under, uh, special circumstances."

Why wait for the wedding? Linda thought, mortified. Why not dig a hole right here? She glared at Tyler, hoping that looks could kill. She had no doubt the minister knew what Tyler had meant by "unusual circumstances."

The minister was studying them intently. "I'm sure the two of you have given this a lot of thought. Just the same, the church offers premarital counseling. I'll sign you up for Tuesday."

"That sounds like a good idea," Linda said. "This way, Tyler and I will get to know each other before we have to live together."

Get to know each other before they have to live together? Had she actually said that? She was on a roll today.

"Thank you, Reverend," Tyler said, "but that won't be necessary. We don't need counseling. We've already made up our minds."

"I'm afraid you don't understand. These sessions are mandatory. It just so happens that I have an opening in next week's group. I don't like to meet with more than four couples at a time. If you decline, the next opening isn't until January."

Tyler looked aghast. "Did you say 'group'? As in group therapy?"

The minister smiled. "It's not as bad as it sounds. All the prospective husbands balk at first, but they soon come to appreciate the benefits. Some couples even form lasting friendships."

Linda nodded. "It's important for a couple to be friends."

"He means with other couples," Tyler said tersely.

She felt like a wire that was strung so tightly it was about to snap. "The next time you feel the need to correct me, I'd appreciate it if you wouldn't do it in public."

"I wasn't correcting you. I was pointing out—"

"You always do that," she accused. "You point things out as if I'm incapable of thinking for myself, and you do it in a way that's not too obvious, which is even worse. It's undermining and manipulative, not to mention patronizing. Like that fiasco with Mark, when we were at the bookstore. Did you think I wouldn't know what you were up to?" She turned to the minister. "Sign us up. It's apparent my fiancé needs counseling."

"The session begins promptly at seven—"

"*I* need counseling? Reverend, she can make a neat freak look like a slob. I've never met a woman so organized."

"What's wrong with being organized? You say the word as if it's blasphemy—oh, excuse me, Reverend, I didn't mean anything by that. That's another thing about him. He refuses to clean up his language."

Tyler rolled his eyes. "Which word do you find offensive? 'Organized' or 'freak'? Anyway, it's true. You're a neat freak. I swear, Reverend—sorry, I didn't mean swear, I meant promise—that with her, every little thing has to be just so. God forbid, pardon the expression, she sees a tiny wrinkle in one of her starchy blouses. It drives her crazy, and that in turn drives *me* crazy. And speaking about driving, do you know what it's like being in a car with her? She gives the term back-seat driver a new definition."

The minister opened his mouth to speak, but Linda beat him to the punch. "You'd be concerned, too," she said to him, "if you saw the way he drives. He thinks just because he's a cop, he can ignore the speed limit."

"Children, please!" the minister interrupted, and the room fell silent. The ticking from the Queen Anne clock was so loud, Linda felt sure it would explode.

The minister clicked his tongue. "As I started to say earlier, the group meets at seven Tuesday evening. In addition, the two of you will be required to go on retreat. This is where you'll talk to each other about your…issues, without a counselor to intervene or any distractions from the outside world. We have a special room set up right here in the church." He looked back down at the book, then raised his head and said, "The room is available next Thursday. Will it be difficult for either of you to take time off from work?"

Tyler frowned. "How much time?"

The minister smiled wryly. "I usually ask the couple to be prepared to spend a full morning or afternoon. But in your case, I must insist on the whole day."

Couples therapy, Tyler thought with disdain. Man bashing would have been a better description. Why was it that the counselors at these things were usually female? "Reverend Nelson must have a cruel streak," he grumbled. "First, he subjects us to couples therapy, and now this."

Linda frowned. "I hope you plan to take this retreat more seriously. Last week, you didn't open your mouth the whole time."

He stared at her in disbelief. "Did you really think I would air my dirty laundry in front of strangers?"

"The idea was to talk about our personal expectations. Not everything is about the Parks empire."

Agitated, Tyler paced the floor. "This place is like a cell. There isn't even a window. What if there's a fire? What if we have to go to the bathroom?"

"The door's not locked," Linda said with exasperation.

"What type of minister shuts off his parishioners from civilization? To think I gave up a full day's work for this farce. Have you seen the remote?"

"Will you please sit down? We need to resolve our differences."

He walked over to the TV and flipped the switch. Nothing. If they weren't allowed to watch TV, why didn't they just remove the damn thing? It wasn't cruel; it was downright sadistic. It was like leaving a pack of cigarettes in front of a person who had just given up smoking. Maybe there was a radio. Hell, he'd even settle for a game of solitaire.

"Tyler, will you please stop pacing? You're making me nervous."

"Everything makes you nervous," he mumbled.

"There, you see? That's exactly what Reverend Nelson was talking about. You're confrontational. Your attitude is one of the problems we need to resolve."

He leaned over and peered into her face. "Okay, I'll play along. But remember, this is a game for two. I'm not the only one here with issues."

"What are you doing?" she asked, flinching under his scrutiny.

"I'm looking for crow's feet. At couples therapy, when I told the group my age, you admitted you were older than me, but you wouldn't say how much."

"What difference does it make?" she asked huffily.

He knew he'd struck a nerve. "It makes no difference to me, but apparently it does to you. Why else would you lie on the marriage license?"

She glared at him. "And how, may I ask, do you know my age?"

"Robert Jackson's report, remember? It's a good thing the license clerk asked for proof of age. This marriage might not be normal, but it's going to be legal."

She stiffened visibly. "There's no need to take that tone. You seem to forget that getting married was your idea in the first place. So if I were you, I'd stop complaining. Unless you want to call the whole thing off, in which case, be my guest."

He sighed, then sank down next to her on the couch. He wished there were someplace else he could sit, like on the other side of the planet. "All right, you want to talk issues, let's talk issues. For starters, what about the living arrangements? I want us to live at my place."

"I told you, it doesn't make sense. Now that Sadie has moved out, I have an extra bedroom."

"You live in an expensive part of town. We won't be able to afford your place on just one salary."

She jutted out her chin. "I don't intend to give up my job."

"You might not have a choice," he reminded her.

Her mouth pulled into a thin line. She obviously

didn't want to enter into a discussion about Walter, which was fine with him. A retreat was one thing; mortal combat was another. But the wedding was next Thursday. They had to resolve their living arrangements before then. "My apartment isn't as large," he said, determined to have his way, "but it'll save us a lot of money."

She looked up at him with dark, beseeching eyes. "I don't care about the money. I care about safety."

Aw, hell. He hated when she got vulnerable on him. It gave her an unfair advantage. His chest tightened, and he took her hand. To his surprise, she didn't pull away. "It's pretty safe where I am downtown," he said, trying to sound reassuring. "I don't have the same fancy video surveillance you have, but there's always a patrol car cruising the streets. And don't forget," he added jauntily, "you're marrying a cop."

"To serve and protect," she said, managing a small smile. "Every cop's motto."

Excitement for their future mounted inside him. "As soon as we've saved enough, we'll make a down payment on a house. It won't be fancy, but it'll be in a safe, clean neighborhood. We'll have a yard in back, maybe a porch out front. I'll build a swing, maybe put in a barbecue. You can plant a garden. I've never had a green thumb, but I'll bet you're a natural."

She hesitated. "I won't deny it, a home like that sounds wonderful. It's the kind of place I used to dream about. The kind of place I used to tell my friends I'd live in when my father came home."

He felt his heart turn over. Maybe there was merit to this retreat business, after all. It looked as if she was finally opening up to him. He knew that to achieve intimacy, they needed to be candid. And intimacy was what he was aiming for—despite her protests against wanting a real marriage. "Tell me about your father," he prodded gently.

"It's no secret. I never knew him. He drove a truck for a living. My mother said that one day, soon after I was born, he set out on a trip across the country, and that was last she saw of him. I'd always hoped he'd return, but when I was fifteen, we heard that his truck had been hijacked and that he'd been killed."

"That must have been tough for you," Tyler said, giving her hand a gentle squeeze. Not only had she never known her father, now her mother and sister were gone, too. "You certainly haven't had an easy time."

She shrugged. "I managed. After I moved out here, I worked as a filing clerk at a leasing company and went to night school to become a CPA. After that, I heard that Parks Fine Jewelry needed an accountant. I arranged for an interview, and Walter hired me on the spot. Apparently, his previous accountant had mysteriously disappeared."

He nodded. "Yes, I know how you came to work for Walter. The report was detailed." Though not detailed enough, he thought, remembering his surprise when she'd told him about Walter's participation in getting Timothy Sands reincarcerated. "You're an amazing woman, Linda. You've accomplished so much. In spite of everything that happened, you didn't let life defeat you."

He pondered how far he could go with this, afraid that if he pushed too hard, she would retreat into herself. Yet how could he expect her to be open when he couldn't return the honesty? It wasn't that he didn't want to; on the contrary, she affected him in a way no one else ever had. In spite of their differences, he related to her on so many levels, particularly when it came to their parents. But he knew he had to hold back. Even though they'd each had a parent who'd been murdered, how could he talk about his past without pointing a finger at Walter? The best he could hope for was a vague kind of communication, something that didn't entail mentioning her boss.

"I can understand a lot of what you must be feeling," he said carefully. "I know what it's like to grow up without a father."

She gave him a small, bleak smile. "My mother always made it clear we were better off without him. She said he wasn't the domestic type, and that no man was."

"Not all men refuse to live up to their responsibilities," he said quietly.

She paused, as though deliberating her next words. "For what it's worth, Tyler, I think you're going to be a good father. You try to come across as hard-boiled, but inside you're a warm and caring person. Maybe a little wounded, but who isn't? You know what I think? I think your past has made you afraid of happiness. You're afraid that once you find it, it'll be snatched away. It's perfectly understandable, given the way you felt while growing up. But you're using Walter like a shield. We both know that he isn't the monster you make him out to be, but to admit that, you'd have to give up your armor."

So much for not mentioning Walter. Tyler didn't want to discuss him, but he saw no way around it. Walter was at the root of their problems. Linda looked up to him, as though he could make up for her growing up fatherless. "You regard Walter as your surrogate parent," he said uneasily.

She surprised him with a smile. "That's what I've been saying all along. I'm so happy you finally see it my way."

Oh, boy. "Linda, I'm going to ask you something and I want you to think carefully before you answer. Believe me when I say this, I'm not trying to upset you."

She looked at him expectantly, a worried expression creasing her brow. "Go ahead."

"Don't you ever question why Walter took you under his wing? He treats you better than he does his own children. You don't think that's strange?"

"No, I don't," she said, her voice taking on a defensive edge. "He's not close to his kids, and he's lonely. You're not the only one who despises him. Can you imagine how he feels? His own children plotting to see him behind bars! I give him what his own children won't—respect and affection. We've maintained an easygoing, nonjudgmental relationship in spite of everything that's happening."

"I'm not sold, but I'm going to let your explanation slide for now. But did you ever ask yourself why he hired you in the first place? You'd just become a CPA. Walter's business is enormously successful. Why would he hire someone so inexperienced?"

"What are you saying? That I'm incompetent?"

"I'm not saying that at all. All I'm saying is that you were like a clean slate. Did you ever think he hired you *because* you were inexperienced?"

"You mean naive," she said dryly. "Let me remind you, you're only twenty-four and you already have your gold shield. Do you think they gave it to you because you're inexperienced?"

"It's not the same thing," Tyler insisted. "Look, forget I said anything. I knew you'd react this way. I shouldn't have brought it up in the first place."

"You're right. You shouldn't have. And you're right about something else. This retreat is a farce. I knew you wouldn't take it seriously. I knew you'd use it as a means to deride Walter. This discussion is over."

She opened her purse and pulled out a paperback. But then she raised her gaze and said, "There's one final matter, however, that we need to resolve. The matter of where you'll be sleeping. If we're going to be living in your apartment, I assume the baby and I will be in the bedroom."

He felt an emptiness in the pit of his stomach. But it wasn't just because of her decision to remain abstinent. He'd accepted that there would be no sex—what choice did he have?—but he'd never considered that they'd be sleeping separately. He'd been looking forward to waking up next to her, seeing her face first thing in the morning. Now it seemed he was to be denied that, as well.

Not bad, Linda thought as she studied herself in the mirror on the bedroom door. The winter-white skirt of her chic designer suit fell just below her knees, accentuating the curve of her calves. Under the stylish collarless jacket, a gold camisole peeked out to match the buttons down the front. Feminine but functional, she decided, pleased with the effect.

"But it's your wedding," Sadie had protested when Linda had told her she was planning to wear the outfit she'd worn to the welcoming party. "You can't wear that dingy bag! You only get married once, hopefully. And I still don't understand why you don't want anyone at the ceremony, anyone meaning *me*. What's this world coming to when you can't even be there when your best friend gets married!"

"If this were going to be a real marriage," Linda had explained for the umpteenth time, "things would be different. I'd be wearing a flowing white gown with a twelve-mile train, and you'd be my matron of honor. But it's not going to be a real marriage, and I won't pretend otherwise. A traditional wedding would be a lie."

Explaining this to someone who had just returned from her honeymoon was an exercise in futility. Sadie had looked so forlorn that, in the end, Linda had agreed to go shopping with her for a suitable outfit. "But nothing traditional," she'd warned her friend.

So far, this whole day was going against tradition, she thought now as she put in her earrings. For one thing, she wasn't surrounded by a flock of bridesmaids trying to conceal her from the groom's gaze, as superstition dictated. Here she was about to get married, alone in her apartment, waiting for Tyler to come by and take her to the church. Not only that, she'd insisted that the ceremony be held late in the day so neither of them would have to miss work. I don't want a fuss, she'd told Sadie. And no fuss was what she was getting.

So why was she fussing over how she looked?

The saying, "Something old, something new, something borrowed, something blue," popped into her head.

Okay, so maybe she didn't want to go down the traditional route, but why tempt fate? She looked down at the shoes she'd bought for the welcoming party. They were two and a half months old; that made them old, right? Her outfit took care of something new. Sadie had lent her a gold beaded bag. That would take care of something borrowed. Now all she needed was something blue.

Something blue, something blue, she mumbled to herself while rummaging through her nightstand drawer. And then she saw the medallion. Suspended from a masculine gold chain, St. Michael's profile was set against a background of blue enamel. "The closest thing to my heart," Tyler had said the night he'd given it to her. At the time, she hadn't realized the significance. St. Michael was the patron saint of policemen. She fastened the chain around her neck and tucked the medallion under her camisole.

Next to the spot where the necklace had lain was a small box. She picked it up. Why not? she thought, opening the carton and removing the lenses. No sense letting them sit around doing nothing.

Fifteen minutes later, she was still struggling with the lenses. How was she supposed to get them in when she couldn't see what she was doing? The buzzer rang, startling her, and when she blinked, the right lens slipped into the corner of her eye. "Oh, gross," she said aloud, then dashed into the hallway.

"You look wonderful," Tyler said moments later, his gaze never leaving her.

"So do you," she said, a flush of heat coursing through her veins. It was the same reaction she'd had when he'd shown up to take her to Sadie's wedding, looking devastatingly handsome in his suit and tie. She gathered her composure. "I can't go."

"It's a little late for second thoughts," he said, visibly disturbed.

"No, you don't understand. One of my lenses is stuck in my eye. I think we should go to the E.R."

He chuckled. "I don't think this exactly constitutes an emergency. Maybe I can help. Come into the kitchen. The light's better there."

In the kitchen, he pulled out a chair from the table and motioned for her to sit. He pulled out another chair and sat facing her. "Now don't move," he said, his fingers gently prying her right eye wide open. "Just one minute. Hold still."

His head was just inches from hers, and his musky aftershave created a heady elixir, sending her senses reeling. She stared straight ahead, trying not to blink.

"There it is. Okay, it's over." He grinned. "No one can accuse me of being inept with my hands. They don't call me Toolman Tyler for nothing."

He'd removed his hands from her face, but his gaze remained unwavering. "What's the matter?" she asked, suddenly alarmed. "Did it fall inside my head or something?"

He laughed. "No, it's in place now, right where it belongs. Can't you tell? You can see clearly, can't you?"

"Oh." So why was he still sitting there? Why was she?

He touched her face again, this time with so much tenderness she thought she would melt. "I wish…" he began, but then stopped abruptly. She knew what he was thinking, and for a brief moment she wished the same thing he did.

If only things were different...

"You're so beautiful," he whispered, his gaze locked on hers. "I can't believe you're going to be my wife."

She averted her eyes. "Tyler, please don't. You're making it difficult."

"Why do you always do that? Why do you look away whenever I compliment you?"

"I guess I'm not used to it," she said with honesty.

"You'd better learn to get used to it, because I intend to spend the rest of my life flattering you."

Something occurred to her that she hadn't thought of before. "Tyler, do you realize how old you'll be when I turn forty?" she asked, horrified.

"Over thirty? Is that too old for you? I guess you'll have to trade me in for a younger man."

"You're incorrigible," she said, smiling.

"Now, that's much better. You know, I'm beginning to think that maybe, just maybe, with a little communication and a truckload of humor, we might be able to make this work."

"I hope so." A silence fell over them, and she stood up. "Well, then," she said uncomfortably, "I guess it's showtime."

She took a look around, and a sadness overcame her. She'd spent so many hours in this room, burning the midnight oil, talking with Sadie. This place held good memories.

Several boxes were stacked along the kitchen walls. More boxes remained in the bedroom, waiting to be taped up and hauled to Tyler's apartment. They'd already moved some of her belongings, and they'd be returning daily until everything was moved, but from this night on she'd be staying at his place. Her lease wasn't up until the end of the year, but thankfully the landlord had allowed her out of the agreement. Sadie had taken only a few pieces of furniture to Frank's place; Linda would be putting what she didn't need into storage, selling it at some later date.

Sadie had been right when she'd called her a pack rat. It was a good thing Linda had the organization gene, or she would be living in chaos. It was amazing how much a person collected over the years. But not all of it was the kind of stuff that could be packed away in boxes. Excess baggage, Sadie had called it. It was time, Linda decided, to let some of it go.

Tyler pulled into the driveway outside his building, then came around to her side.

"Aren't you coming up?" Linda asked. "What about dinner?"

He planted a kiss on her nose. "'Fraid not, sweetheart. No time. Got a stakeout tonight. I'll change my clothes at the station. But don't worry, the freezer is full. Lots of microwave dinners in there, since I know you don't like to cook. I should be home by midnight."

She felt oddly disappointed. She would have thought that tonight, of all nights, he would have made an effort to be with her. Maybe theirs was just a marriage of convenience, but he might have shown a little consideration. Just because they'd decided not to have sex didn't mean they couldn't spend the evening together. "You only get married once," Sadie had said. Linda frowned, recalling how her friend had qualified the statement with a flippant "hopefully."

She unlocked the door to the apartment and turned off the alarm. At her insistence, Tyler had installed a keypad system. She sighed. It was better than nothing, but it wasn't the security she'd hoped for. What was the use of marrying a cop if he wasn't around to protect her?

She changed into jeans and a sweatshirt and set about making dinner. Tyler hadn't been kidding about the freezer—it was jam-packed with prepared dinners. She pulled out a chicken potpie. A bottle of chardonnay on the counter caught her eye, and for a moment she was tempted. If she weren't pregnant, she wouldn't have hesitated. Wasn't a wedding toast in order?

The evening passed with agonizing slowness. She tried to read, but couldn't concentrate. She turned on the TV, then clicked it off. She thought about calling Sadie, but decided against it. She couldn't keep running to her best friend every time she felt out of sorts. She was a big girl now, a married woman.

She went into the bedroom to unpack the boxes she and Tyler had brought over yesterday. Clicking her tongue, she picked up a pair of his socks from the floor. She hadn't said anything about the clutter in the living room—why on earth did a person need so many remotes?—but if the bedroom was going to be hers, he might have made an attempt to tidy it. As she was dusting the bureau, a silver gift bag caught her eye. A present from Sadie, she remembered. "Guaranteed to make your wedding night memorable," the card had read.

She pulled out the teeniest, flimsiest nightgown she'd ever seen. She examined it closely—what there was of it. Good grief, you could practically see right through it! Did women actually wear these things? It certainly wasn't practical. Her idea of sleepwear was a cotton nightgown in the summer, flannel pj's when it was cold.

Sadie was hopeless. Linda had been adamant about not wanting to wear something traditional to the wedding ceremony, so what did her friend go and do? She bought her something traditional for the wedding night. Traditional according to Sadie. Linda had always believed that the wedding night should be elegant and romantic, not something out of an X-rated movie. Not that there would have been a *real* wedding night, even if Tyler had stayed home.

She thought about the wedding. She hadn't wanted a fuss, and no fuss was what she'd gotten. At six o'clock, only one week after the retreat, Reverend Nelson had ushered them into the chapel, and by six-fifteen it was over. It's amazing how in just a short time an entire life could change. One minute, she'd been Miss Linda Mailer, single; the next minute, Mrs. Tyler Carlton, married. "Married," she repeated to herself, over and over. If you said it often enough, it seemed to lose its meaning.

"You don't regret doing it this way?" Tyler had asked when they'd pulled out of the parking lot behind the church. His voice had been tinged with disappointment. "The ceremony was so cold, so impersonal. It left me feeling empty."

"You know I hate fusses." But in truth, she'd felt let down, too. To be honest, it would have been a comfort for her to have had Sadie by her side. The matron of honor had been the minister's secretary; the best man, his bookkeeper. And, Linda had to admit, it might have been nice to have some sort of celebration dinner following the service. Getting married wasn't something you did every day.

"I never really believed that marriage could be just an arrangement," Tyler had commented on the way home, his gaze on the road ahead. "The ceremony really drove it home."

After that, he'd remained quiet, and she'd thought, What happened to "a little communication and a truckload of humor"?

"Told you so," she imagined her mother saying. Audrey Mailer's austere face rose in her mind. If my mother had been a little less rigid, a little more understanding, Linda wondered, would my father have stayed?

She didn't want Tyler to leave her. She didn't want to be alone. But her fear of being alone wasn't the only reason she wanted him to stay. He made her feel wanted. Made her feel beautiful. She'd liked the way he'd looked at her after helping with her contact lenses. She'd liked the way his eyes had gleamed when she'd said, "I do."

The nightgown felt soft and slinky in her hands. She fingered the delicate lace on the bodice, reminding herself that what she was planning had nothing to do with the way he made her feel.

What she was planning was a compromise—a compromise and an investment in her future. Call it a compromise, call it an investment, but any way she looked at it, tonight was her wedding night. What she was planning wasn't something she'd make a habit of, but once in a while wouldn't kill her.

She stripped off her clothing and slipped into the sexy garment. She glanced at herself in the mirror but, embarrassed at what she saw, she averted her gaze. This isn't you, she reminded herself. This is just a role.

She lay on the bed, waiting for his return. In minutes, she felt herself dozing. She dreamed she was standing outside her mother's house, watching as police cars arrived, listening to the sirens as they wailed in the night.

She jerked awake. Moments later, she heard Tyler's key in the lock, and she darted into the adjoining bathroom to freshen up. What she saw in the mirror shocked her, but she didn't turn her head away. Intrigued, she peered at the reflection. Was that really her?

Lyla.

She shook out her hair, smiled wickedly at her image and returned to the bedroom.

Chapter Seven

"Hi," Tyler said awkwardly, his back turned to her as he rummaged through a drawer in the dresser. He felt like a stranger in his own home. "I'll just be a minute. I suppose I should move some of my things to the living room, since that's where I'll be sleeping." He shut the drawer, turned around—and his mouth dropped open.

"What's the matter, baby?" Linda asked, smiling suggestively. "Cat got your tongue? That would be most regrettable," she added, licking her lips.

"Linda, are you feeling okay?" He didn't know what he'd expected when he'd come home, but he hadn't expected this. Why was she dressed in that tiny nightgown? Not that he was complaining. The way she looked made his pulse fly straight off the charts. He might be confused, but he certainly wasn't unhappy.

"Come to Mama," she purred. "No, stay there. Mama's going to come to you." She sashayed over to him, and he realized that the fabric of her gown wasn't flesh tone; it was transparent. He stood there staring, and she laughed.

She looked him over seductively. "Well, Detective, are you just going to stand there, or are you going to show me some action? Or maybe you should arrest me. I'm about to do something illicit."

So, she wanted to play. Hell, if fantasy was what she wanted, fantasy was what he'd give her. "What do you have in mind?" he asked, moving his fingers slowly across her breasts.

"Bad boy," she mock-scolded. "Keep that up, and I'll have to put you in handcuffs."

Whoa. Handcuffs? Was this the same woman who'd given him advance warning not to kiss her when the minister pronounced them married? "I don't like public displays of affection," she'd explained primly. Public? The minister, his secretary and his bookkeeper had been their entire audience.

An unsettling feeling began to stir inside him. "Linda," he said gently, "you don't have to do this."

"Do what?" she asked, feigning ignorance. "This?" She trickled her lips along his cheek. "Or this?" she asked, then teased his ear with her tongue. "How about this?" She wrapped her arms around his neck, pressing herself against him.

Her endeavors didn't go unnoticed. In spite of his misgivings, he felt himself growing hard against her stomach. He drew her into a full embrace, and she arched her back in response. But when he tried to ease her toward the bed, she refused to budge.

"Let's not be conventional," she said huskily. "I want to initiate the room properly. What I suggest," she murmured while nibbling on the corner of his mouth, "is that we start on the floor, then work our way to the bureau. After that, Detective, if you still have energy, we'll do the bed. I intend to convert this room into our little playroom."

Suddenly, her hands were everywhere at once—unbuttoning his shirt, unfastening his belt, unzipping his trousers. She reached inside, and he let out a gasp.

"We have all night, honey," he said, gently moving her hands aside. "Do you think we can take it just a little slower?"

And then, silence. The fire in her eyes died, and she backed away. When she finally spoke, her voice was cold. "Take it a little slower? Why? Isn't this what you want?"

"Linda, please. I'm sorry. I didn't mean—"

"You didn't mean what?" she lashed out. She turned her head away. "Oh, God. I feel like such a fool. Oh, God."

"Linda, no." He reached for her, but she jerked away. She pulled a bathrobe from the closet and then rushed out of the bedroom, slamming the door behind her.

Aw, hell, he thought, plopping down on the bed. He'd sure bungled that. Talk about being insensitive. He knew his words had hurt her, had realized it as soon as they were out of his mouth. Only, he wasn't sure why. All he'd done was suggest that they slow down, but she'd acted as if she'd been mortally wounded.

He couldn't figure her out. Dammit, he was a cop. He was supposed to be good at figuring things out. But

Linda was something else. She was an enigma he just couldn't solve.

One thing he did know, she felt something for him. She'd responded to him too many times for him to think otherwise. The problem was, she wouldn't follow through.

He didn't want to pressure her, but a man could dream, couldn't he? He'd believed it was just a matter of time before she gave in to her feelings, and she'd made him think that tonight was the night.

He changed out of his clothes, into a T-shirt and sweatpants. Normally he liked to sleep in his boxers, but under the circumstances it wasn't a good idea. He supposed he'd have to go shopping for pajamas.

He deliberated going into the living room. He didn't know what was wrong—all he knew was that somehow he had to fix it. He and Linda needed to talk. If they wanted their marriage to work, they'd need to work out their problems.

He opened the bedroom door to a dimly lit room. Her presence was everywhere. Her coat was on a hook by the front door. Her books now joined his in the bookcase. The Picasso from her bedroom hung on the wall by the window.

He remembered when he'd hung the print a few days ago. "A little to the left," she'd instructed. "No, that's too much. More to the right. A little higher. No, lower."

"I don't get it," he'd said, staring at the picture after she'd finally made up her mind. Two misshapen figures loomed down at him from the wall. He could have hung it upside down, and it would have made just as much sense.

"Things aren't always what they appear to be," she'd said in a cryptic voice.

He entered the living room. Curled up under a throw on the futon, she was watching TV. He felt a tug at his heartstrings. She was sniffling into a tissue.

"Care for some company?" he asked gently. When she didn't answer, he sat down beside her. "What are you watching?"

"*Shrek*," she managed through her tears. "It's one of my f-favorite m-movies. I must have seen it a d-dozen times."

"It's one of my favorites, too. That's why I bought it. I think the animation is brilliant." He smiled. "I never would have thought you'd enjoy a movie about an ugly ogre who lives in a swamp, eats slime and makes candles from his ear wax."

"B-but this one…this one is s-so…s-sweet." She blew her nose daintily into a tissue.

Tyler shook his head. She was an enigma, all right. One minute, she was seducing him; the next minute, she was crying over a children's movie.

"It's very clever," he said, settling back on the couch. "I like the way they weave in the fairy tales. It's a fairy tale, too, in a way."

He didn't want to sit here and talk about fairy tales. He wanted to talk about what had happened in the bedroom. But afraid she would retreat into herself, he held back.

"It's not your typical fairy tale," she said, wiping the moisture from her face. "Fiona is one smart cookie, and tough, too. But not only that, she has a dark secret."

He was afraid to move, afraid to touch her. He remained next to her, wishing he had a magic wand that would make all their problems disappear. He knew she was hurting; he just didn't know how to help her. He felt her pain as acutely as if it were his own.

Maybe he could weave the subject into the conversation, the way the movie had woven in the fairy tales. But he'd have to be a little more subtle, he thought, recalling his contrived conversation with Mark at the café. She'd seen through that ploy right off the bat. "Fiona can only realize her true self once she finds true love," he said softly.

Suddenly, she looked up at him and asked, "Do you believe in happy endings?"

The question caught him off guard. "I believe in doing the right thing," he said.

She smiled sadly. "They're not always the same thing."

"No, not always, but if you don't try to do what's right, you'll never find happiness. How can a person be happy knowing he deliberately set out to do something wrong?"

"I guess some people have no conscience." She regarded him steadily. "What if you believe you're doing the right thing, but the right thing turns out to be wrong?"

"What do you mean?" he asked cautiously.

"You believe that Walter is guilty, and I believe he's innocent. We're each acting on our own belief. According to you, if either of us acted any differently, it would be wrong. How can we both be right?"

So, he thought, disappointed, she wasn't talking about what had happened in the bedroom. Funny how the conversation always returned to Walter. He sighed. "Sometimes a belief evolves erroneously. Sometimes we need to reevaluate the evidence."

His answer must have appeased her, because she nodded. "Spoken like a true lawman. But I know what you mean. I know how easily impressions can change." She hesitated. "When I first joined the company, I thought it would be the perfect place to work. It was so cold, so impersonal."

He grimaced. Those were the two words he'd used to describe their wedding. "Go on," he said tentatively. What was she getting at?

"Parks Fine Jewelry is a huge, successful business, and I thought I could lose myself in the work. The last thing I wanted was to form any attachments. But as time went by, I grew close to Walter. He was there for me when Timothy Sands was released from prison." She straightened the coverlet on her legs. "Here's the thing. Even if I turned out to be wrong—which won't happen—how could I turn my back on the man who saved my life? If Timothy hadn't gone back to prison, he would have come after me. No matter the circumstances, it would be wrong for me to turn against Walter after what he did for me."

"They say that the road to hell is paved with good intentions," Tyler said tightly, then immediately regretted his words. Here she was opening up to him, and he had to go and get judgmental.

Her eyes flashed with anger. Or was it hurt? He couldn't tell. She sat rigidly on the couch, not responding to his remark.

"I'm sorry," he said with sincerity. "I didn't mean to sound harsh." He tried another tack. "But how can you be so sure you're right? You don't have all the facts. You're a smart woman, Linda. I can't believe you'd base your convictions on blind faith alone. You know what I think? I think you've been doubting Walter all along, but you won't admit it."

"Let me remind you," she snapped, "that in this country, a person is innocent until proven guilty."

Dammit, why couldn't he learn to keep his mouth shut? He might just as well have accused her of being Walter's accomplice. When it came to her boss, she was closed-minded.

They watched the rest of the movie in silence. After the last scene, in which a whole horde of fairy-tale creatures came together to celebrate the marriage of Shrek and Fiona, Linda rose and said, "And on that happy ending, I think I'll call it a night. Do you need help making up your bed?"

"No, I'm fine. I'll get the linen from the closet. Good night, Linda."

The bedroom door closed behind her, and he aimed the remote at the TV. He clicked the off button, and the picture died.

And that's that, he thought. Happy endings were only for fairy tales.

"I want to do what's right," the woman said over the phone. "I have something that belongs to you. Ronald wanted you to have it, and I aim to give it to you."

"I don't understand. Who are you?" Not wanting to be overheard, Linda spoke in a hushed tone. Laughter wafted into her office through the open doorway. The day was winding to a close.

"I told you. The name's Charlene. Charlene Butler, Ronald Pritchard's girlfriend. He said he had something you'd be interested in, something to do with the business. But if you want it, come get it. I did my part. I called you."

"Isn't he dead?" Linda blurted. The only thing she knew of the man was that he'd disappeared more than five years ago, shortly before she'd started working for Walter. The papers had linked his disappearance to organized crime. Apparently he'd been involved in some serious gambling. It had been reported that he'd been shot and killed for not paying back what he owed.

"Of course he's dead," the woman said. "Why else would I be calling you? But like I said, I done my part. You want what's yours, you come by the Starlite Lounge. Be there at eight. I ain't calling again."

"Where is this place?" Linda asked, apprehension filling her.

"It's on Market Street, west of 6th."

Linda frowned. She knew the neighborhood. "I still don't understand—" She heard a click, then found herself listening to a dial tone.

She put down the phone, mulling over the strange conversation. What did Walter's previous accountant have to do with her? What could he possibly have wanted her to have? If it was related to the business, why hadn't Charlene contacted Walter instead?

Must have been a crank call, she decided. Since this whole thing started, she'd been getting one after another. She grimaced. She could just imagine herself traipsing out to Market and 6th. Not exactly one of San Francisco's finer districts.

She pushed the conversation from her mind. Unable to concentrate on work, she allowed her thoughts to drift to last night. Every time she recalled the scene in the bedroom, she felt like disappearing into thin air. She pictured herself the way she imagined Tyler had seen her. Cheap. Tawdry. She'd believed she was offering him what he wanted, but apparently she'd been wrong. Take it a little slower, he'd said. Every time she recalled those words, her face burned with humiliation.

"Linda?"

Startled, she looked up to see cool, brown eyes staring down at her. How long had Walter been standing at her desk? How long had she been lost in thought?

"Walter," she acknowledged, feeling flushed. He leaned his tall, athletic frame in close, glancing at the papers scattered on her desk. Noting the grim look on his leathery tanned face, she sighed deeply.

He knew. He knew about her marriage.

She hadn't really believed he wouldn't find out. It was inevitable. The Parks network, Tyler had called the family. He'd told her he was planning to tell Cade and Emily, but she hadn't thought he'd tell them so soon. Heavens, she hadn't even been married one full day! She was surprised that no one knew about the pregnancy. Or maybe everyone did, but they were too polite to mention it. She could just imagine them talking in whispers behind her back.

"I wanted to wish you all the best," Walter said. "With everything that's been happening around here, I know we haven't had much time to talk, but to tell you the truth, I'm a little hurt you didn't even mention you were seeing Tyler, let alone planning to marry him. One other thing troubles me, as well. I don't understand why you showed up at work today."

He means he doesn't understand why I haven't quit, she thought. "Walter, let me assure you that I'll never let my marriage interfere with my work," she said carefully. She wanted to add, "Or with us," but that wouldn't be the truth. How could it be? Tyler and Walter were blood enemies.

He gave her a quizzical look. "I meant, I'd thought you'd be off somewhere on a honeymoon."

"Oh. I thought—"

He held up his hand. "I know what you thought. But you were wrong. I have no intention of letting you go. You're a good girl. You're loyal and hardworking. I trust you, and these days, a little trust goes a long way. All I want is for you to be happy. I'd hate to see you get hurt." He hesitated, then turned to leave. "Good night, Linda. Enjoy your weekend. I'll see you Monday morning."

Coat in hand, he left her office. A few more good-byes trickled in from the corridor, and then there was quiet. She swiveled in her chair to stare out the window. As touched as she was by Walter's concern, she couldn't help but wonder why he hadn't fired her. If I were in his shoes, she thought, *I* would fire me. "A little trust goes a long way," he'd said. How could he trust the woman who'd married his enemy?

Keep your friends close and your enemies closer.

Stop it, she ordered herself. This is all Tyler's doing. He's turned you into a paranoid mess.

She didn't want to believe that Walter was guilty. Didn't want to believe that someone who'd been so good to her could have committed those heinous crimes.

She had to learn the truth. Had to know which side of the fence to sit on, as Tyler had put it. The uncertainty was making her crazy, causing her to doubt everything anyone told her. If she didn't find out once and for all, she'd end up losing them both.

Maybe this Charlene character was on the level. Maybe she had information regarding Walter, information that could lead to the truth. Talking to her was worth a shot.

Linda had told Tyler she was planning to work late, and he'd said he'd be working, too. The stakeout last night had been unsuccessful, and he and Nick were going to try again. He'd said not to expect him home until midnight.

She had no reason to tell him she'd changed her plans.

After a quick dinner at the apartment, she rummaged through her closet, looking for something to wear. She couldn't show up at a place called the Starlite Lounge looking like a prude. If just the prospect of going alone to a bar made her feel uncomfortable, what would looking conspicuous do? You have to blend in, her mother always said. If no one notices you, you can't get hurt.

She brushed aside her oversize dresses and skirts with a sweep of her hand. Maybe Sadie was right. Maybe she needed a livelier wardrobe. Another thought came to her, this one making her smile. Soon, all these clothes would fit just fine. Not that she intended to wear them. Just because she was pregnant didn't mean she had to look frumpy. She laughed out loud. She was beginning to sound like Sadie.

Maybe this weekend she'd do a little shopping. But

what about the problem at hand? She needed something now. What could she wear that wouldn't make her stand out like a clothed woman on a nude beach?

Her gaze fell on the black leather skirt she'd worn the night she'd met Tyler. Why not? she thought. She'd wear the little halter top, too. That and some makeup, and she'd fit right in. Besides, it could be fun. Kind of like being in disguise. She felt a rush of excitement. Was this how Tyler felt when he went undercover? Okay, so she wasn't a cop, and Charlene seemed to know exactly who she was, but she was out to get information. Why not get in the spirit?

This time, she had no trouble putting in her lenses. That done, she applied her makeup and studied herself in the mirror. She smiled. Nancy Drew she wasn't.

She glanced at her watch. It was already after seven. I'd better get a move on, she thought, envisioning driving around and around, looking for a parking space. She had no intention of walking any great distance in that neighborhood. If she had to, she'd circle the block until she found a spot right out front. Eight o'clock, Charlene had said. Linda didn't want to be late and risk missing her. She grabbed her coat and headed for the door.

The parking fairy must have been in a good mood, because there was an empty spot just outside the lounge. In fact, the whole block was empty. This place sure is popular, Linda thought, grimacing. Well, if hardly anyone showed up, at least she wouldn't feel inconspicuous. Which meant she wouldn't have to remove her coat to display her skimpy outfit. Tugging the coat close to her body, she glanced at the neon sign above the door. Some of the letters had burned out, and the sign read, THE TAR T LOUNGE.

She was a half hour early. Now what was she supposed to do? If the inside of the lounge was as seedy as the outside, she was in deep trouble. No way would she sit in there, alone, for thirty minutes.

She decided to wait in the car. A man in a torn, scruffy coat teetered down the sidewalk, stopping to look at her through the passenger window. She averted her eyes. Oh, God. What was she doing here?

She counted to ten, then stole a glance out of the corner of her eye. Even though he was gone, her uneasiness hadn't abated. She couldn't just stay out here like a sitting duck. A cold fear swept through her. Sure, the doors were locked, but someone could smash a window, right? What if he had a gun? Well, that answered that. She was going in.

She drew in her breath and made a dash for the lounge. Inside, she couldn't see much. The only lighting came from the fluorescent lamp in the ceiling above the bar and from the lanterns on the small round tables. It didn't take her long to realize that they weren't lanterns; they were small lamps in the shape of topless hula dancers.

She headed straight for the back of the room and sat at a table. Her eyes now accustomed to the dimness, she could make out the tan Leatherette stools at the bar. A man in a dirty overcoat sat alone, drinking from a bottle. Next to the cash register behind the bar, a woman in a red bustier was reading a newspaper.

Linda fidgeted nervously in her chair. The wood frame creaked. The woman looked up, folded the paper and approached her. "Don't know why anyone reads that rag," she said. "First they say that Elvis came back from the dead, and now they say he's the father of quadruplets. Yeah, right. Quadruplets! What can I get you, sugar?"

"Um, nothing, thank you," Linda said, fascinated. The woman, who appeared to be in her mid-forties, looked like an aging dancehall girl straight out of a fifties' TV western. Her bleached blond hair was teased into a beehive; her makeup was so heavy she could have been wearing a mask.

"If you're going to sit here all night on your fanny, you're going to have to order something."

"Um, I'm waiting for someone."

"I just bet you are. Look, sugar, if you're not going to order something, you're going to have to take your business somewhere else."

Good Lord, did the woman think she was a prostitute? "A Coke," Linda answered, flustered. "Diet, in a tall glass with two cubes of ice. And a twist of lemon. No, make that a ginger ale. With two cubes of ice. But no lemon."

"Lady, you winding me up? I got no time for gags. I'm a busy person, in case you haven't noticed."

No time? The man at the bar was the only customer in the place. "I'm sorry. I won't take up any more of your time than necessary. Maybe you can help me. I'm waiting for a person named Charlene Butler. Would you happen to know her?"

To her surprise, the woman sat down next to her. "I'm Charlene Butler. You're early, Mailer."

"I'm sorry."

"Would you stop saying you're sorry?"

"Okay. Sorry."

Charlene rolled her eyes. "Look, why don't we get right to the point? Like I said on the phone, Ronald is dead. When I went through his papers, I found this." She pulled out a small crumpled envelope from the pocket of her tight black skirt and handed it to Linda. "It's got your name on it."

Something else was written on the envelope, as well. Scribbled under Linda's name were the words, "Upon my death." She looked back up at Charlene. "What's in it?"

Charlene looked insulted. "Do I look like the type who reads other people's mail? Besides, I don't want to know. Most likely, it has something to do with what's been in the papers, and I don't want to get involved. But I know Ronald wanted you to have this. I did what he wanted, and that's the end of it for me."

The man at the bar turned around on his stool and called, "Charlie! Get your fanny over here and bring me another beer!" With a shock, Linda realized that he was the same man who'd peered into her car.

"Hold your horses!" Charlene called back, hurrying over to the bar. "I'm coming!"

Linda tore open the envelope. She pulled out a yellowed piece of paper and examined it closely. Dated more than twenty-five years ago, it was a receipt made out to Parks Fine Jewelry for a safe-deposit box. She didn't recognize the name of the bank, yet a strange feeling passed through her, as if she'd come across this document before.

She chewed her lip, trying to remember. What was it about the receipt that seemed familiar? And then it came to her. Last August, when she'd been alone in Walter's home office reconciling his personal accounts, she'd come across another receipt dated twenty-five years ago. Only, that one had mentioned uncut diamonds and the name Van Damon. Thinking that the receipt had been misfiled, she'd tucked it in her purse, intending to file it properly at the office downtown. But she'd found no records there for Van Damon. She'd meant to ask Walter about it, but instead, she'd locked it away in her desk. She hadn't thought it important enough to probe further, but now, with the second receipt in hand, her curiosity was piqued. She knew that a lot of data had been archived. Maybe she'd been looking in the wrong place.

At the time, she hadn't questioned why she hadn't gone to Walter. Maybe Tyler was right. Maybe she'd been suspicious of her boss all along, but hadn't wanted to admit it.

The archives were located in the utility room across from her office. Although the room was kept locked, some of the employees, herself included, had a key. But hardly anyone ever went in there. If someone saw her searching through the dusty old boxes, he might become suspicious. She didn't want anyone asking questions.

No time like the present, she thought. Even though the jewelry store on the ground floor would be open until nine, she knew she'd be alone upstairs. She'd been the last to leave.

She placed the bank receipt into her purse. On her way to the entrance, she waved at Charlene. Charlene ignored her, but the man at the bar gave her a lewd smile. "It's a rough world out there, doll," he said as Linda passed by. "I'd hate to see you get hurt."

She gasped. Those were the very words that Walter had used.

Still feeling unnerved, she arrived at Union Square twenty minutes later. Most of the major department stores, as well as numerous art galleries, shops and cafés, were within walking distance from the square, and even though it was almost eight, the trendy district was bustling with shoppers.

She had a permit for the garage on Post Street, but she didn't like parking there at night. After working late, she never left the office without her pepper spray in hand. This must be my lucky day, she thought as she approached the jewelry store. Silently blessing the parking fairy, she pulled into a vacant spot just outside the store.

She considered taking the outdoor stairs up to the offices, just as she did every morning before the store opened. But she wanted to alert the security guard that she'd returned, so she decided to take the indoor stairwell at the back of the showroom.

"Evenin', Linda," the night guard said. "Thanks for the batch of cookies you left for me the other night. Loved the new recipe, and so did the missus." His smile faded, and he looked at her with disapproval. "Burning the midnight oil again, I see. How many times does that make it this month? They're working you too hard. After a full day, you shouldn't be stuck here in this place. You should be out having fun with your new husband. Congratulations, by the way. I hear he's a fine man."

Word certainly traveled fast. Why was she surprised?

The Parks network wasn't limited to family; it extended to Walter's employees.

"Thank you, George. Yes, Tyler is a fine man, and you're right, I work too hard. But you know how it goes. Every business has a busy season. Thanksgiving and Christmas are just around the corner."

But it wasn't the approaching holidays that had been taking up her time. Because of the upcoming audit, she'd been swamped with work. Even though she hated being alone upstairs—no one else ever stayed late, not even Walter, who disappeared every day at five with his secretary—she felt she had no choice. There were only so many hours in a day. She never would have had the nerve to stay alone if not for the night guard downstairs. He was just a panic button away.

She smiled at him, then said, "Fine evening to you, too, George. I have some paperwork to go over, but I'll be long gone before midnight." Truth was, she didn't know how long she'd be there. She wasn't even sure what she was looking for.

Something occurred to her as she climbed the stairs. What if she found something incriminating? Would she confront Walter?

She chided herself for being such a worrywart. She felt sure she wouldn't find anything, that her sleuthing would prove fruitless. She might have abandoned the whole scheme if not for the words on the envelope, *Upon my death.* Ronald had been gone more than five years. Why had Charlene waited until now to contact her?

At the top of the stairs she entered the code for the alarm, then opened the door and stepped into the corridor. She switched on the lights. The place always looks so different at night, she thought with a shudder. Her heart pounding, she went directly to her office.

She hung up her coat on the hook on her door. At her desk, she fired up her computer, then pulled out the receipt from her purse. She checked through the account database, but found no reference to the bank in question. She searched through the filing cabinet. There, too, she came up empty-handed.

She opened the drawer to her desk. The receipt for the uncut diamonds lay just where she'd left it, in an envelope tucked beneath her memo pad. She left her office and went to the utility room.

A bulb hanging from the ceiling provided the only light. She found the box for the year in question and began leafing through the files. Outside the room, a phone rang, and she froze. Afraid to let anyone know she was there alone, she never answered the phone at night. She held her breath until the service picked up, then continued with her search.

The archives contained no reference to either receipt. In fact, not one dossier, memo or any other paperwork had been filed for the entire month of July. She knew that the archives were by no means complete, but she found it odd that July was the only month missing from this particular box.

She glanced at the receipts again, thinking she might have misread them. But no, she hadn't been mistaken. Both were dated twenty-five years ago, one July 11, the other July 26. Disheartened, she placed the box back onto its shelf.

A beeping echoed in the corridor, and her pulse

jumped. The fax machine, she realized, and let out a nervous laugh. Giddy with relief and feeling a little foolish, she turned off the light and left the storeroom. She closed the door and locked it behind her. Once back in her office, she decided to look up Van Damon on the Internet. She groaned. The screen had come back with thousands of hits. She keyed in "diamonds." This time only one item popped up, and she clicked on the link. What she learned startled her. Van Damon was a Dutch warlord living in Africa. One of his many illegal activities included smuggling uncut diamonds into the States. She didn't want to believe that Walter was involved, but what other explanation could there be for the receipt?

She powered down the computer. The humming from the processor ceased, and an eerie silence fell over the room. Eerie not because it was nighttime, but because something felt different. Something felt wrong.

I'd hate to see you get hurt.

Nervously, she lifted her gaze, and a piercing scream sliced through the stillness.

The scream, she realized, was hers.

Chapter Eight

The room was spinning. She began shaking, her heart started racing and she broke into a cold sweat. She felt all the color drain from her face.

You...

Forcing herself to breathe slowly, she tried to recall the words she'd need to help her get past the anxiety.

...will not die. You will get through this, no matter how bad you feel.

Tyler rushed to her side. "Linda, are you all right?" His voice sounded muffled above the ringing in her ears. "I'm so sorry. I didn't mean to scare you."

She wanted to tell him not to worry, that this had happened before and it would soon pass. But her breath was coming in ragged hiccups, and she could hardly speak. "C-can't breathe," she finally managed. She leaned forward in her chair, gripping the armrests. "Ch-chest hurts."

It's not the situation that's bothering you. It's all in your thinking.

She hated feeling this way. It had been years since she'd had a relapse. Yet even though her mind was draped in haze, she was able to discern the difference between this panic attack and all the others before it. The other attacks had arisen from fear; this one, strangely, had sprouted from relief.

Stay in the present. There's no danger.

Tyler's face slowly came into focus. Standing next to her, he eased her head against him and gently stroked her forehead.

When she'd seen the shadow outside her office door, her first response had been to scream. Only after he'd called her name and she'd realized who he was did the attack take hold. It was a delayed reaction, but frightening nonetheless. Her heartbeat could attest to that.

You are strong. You are brave.

She closed her eyes and, leaning into him, gave in to his touch. He had a way about him that was gentle and healing. His hands, soft and rough at the same time, felt cool against her skin, like balm on sunburn. She was reminded of that night on the beach when dizziness had overtaken her and he'd held her until it had subsided. Except back then, she'd been feeling the symptoms of pregnancy; this was different. This is what happens when you're caught off guard, she thought, chiding herself for her weakness. Not only did she hate feeling helpless, she hated when anyone saw her this way.

The revolving room finally came to a stop, and her breathing returned to normal. Embarrassed, she pushed his hand away and forced herself to an upright position.

"What are you doing here?" Her question came out as an accusation.

"Better not make any sudden moves," he said in a worried voice.

"You sound like a cop," she said dryly. "Do I look like a suspect?"

He winced at her tone. "I meant, I wouldn't want you to pass out."

"Oh, you'd just love that," she retorted. "It would give you the opportunity to play Mr. Macho when you scoop me up in your arms. Let me remind you that it's your fault I felt this way to begin with. You scared me half to death!"

To her surprise, amusement crossed his face. "You're saying I came up here deliberately to scare you just so I could make you feel better afterward?" He narrowed his eyes. "Why are you so gussied up?"

"Leave my clothes out of this," she admonished. "What you did tonight was just a repeat performance. What about what happened at the welcoming party? It was because of you I fainted. You can't imagine the shock I felt when I saw you. You must have felt like a real hero, rescuing the damsel in distress in front of a full audience."

His eyes were bright with mirth. "Now you're saying I shouldn't have gone to a party that was being held in my honor? I should have realized that you—a woman I knew only as Lyla Sinclair—would be there, and knowing this, I should have declined?" A wry smile came to his lips. "You must be clairvoyant. How did you know what I was feeling when you fainted?"

"What?"

"You said I must have felt like a hero. How could you know how I felt? You were out cold."

"Don't twist my words, Tyler. You know what I meant."

"Now you're saying that *I'm* clairvoyant?"

"You know, you missed your true calling. You should have been a lawyer. All I'm saying is that I resent the way you use me to pump up your ego, especially since you're the one who gets me in these predicaments to begin with."

"It was your decision to work late, not mine." His expression stilled. "That man works you too hard."

"Leave Walter out of this. I'm talking about the pregnancy. If I weren't having a baby, I wouldn't be feeling queasy all the time, and you wouldn't be playing nursemaid."

"Now you're blaming morning sickness on me? All this time I thought nature was the culprit. As for your getting pregnant, I wasn't alone in the room when our child was conceived, or have you conveniently forgotten that, too?"

"No, I have not," she said in a huff. "All I meant was that you seem to relish my weakness."

He threw up his arms as if in surrender. "Fine. You win. If you want to play the martyr, go ahead. Only do it alone." He headed for the door.

"Tyler, wait."

He turned back to her and frowned. "Why? Is there something else you'd like to pin on me?"

"I'm, um, feeling better now."

"Glad to hear it," he said sarcastically. "Except now I feel like hell."

"Tyler?"

His frown deepened. "What?"

"I'm sorry."

He sighed audibly. "Must be hormones."

Must be, she silently concurred. Why else would she be acting this way? It seemed that whenever she was with him, all she wanted to do was pick a fight. Hormones or not, she had no right to keep haranguing him. "I do tend to relegate blame, don't I?" she said apologetically. "And about that macho thing—I don't mind, not really."

A slow grin spread across his face. "Nah, you're right. Sometimes I get a little carried away. Sometimes I forget I'm not a superhero."

She laughed at that, then quickly sobered. "It's an admirable trait, wanting to save the world. I shouldn't have snapped at you. It's just that lately almost everything seems to set me off. Maybe you're right. Maybe it's hormonal. I never used to be this way. Even as a child, I was complacent." A memory took hold, and a sadness filled her.

"What is it?" he asked, looking at her with concern.

"Just something I remembered. My mother used to park me in the corner and forget all about me—I was so quiet, you wouldn't even know I was in the room. I'd watch her as she went about her work in the kitchen. I wouldn't take my eyes off her, for fear of her disappearing."

"You miss her," he said simply.

Did she? She wasn't sure. "My mother was a stern woman, with unbending rules. She became even stricter when my sister ran off to get married. But I didn't complain. She was a single parent, raising me the best she could. I admit it wasn't easy living with her, but she was my mother. I loved her. I didn't realize how much until it was too late. I fell apart when she died. And then, losing my sister... For a long time after, I felt incapable of taking care of myself. Oh, I don't mean functionally. I went through the motions. I did what I had to do. I mean emotionally. But time is a great healer, and I became stronger. I just never got over being afraid. But I'm tired of letting fear control my life. I'm tired of depending on others to make me feel safe."

She stopped suddenly. Those last two statements had sounded like a declaration of independence, and that surprised her. When had self-reliance become so important?

Then something occurred to her. As safe and secure as she'd felt in Tyler's arms, it had been her own doing, her self-talk and forced composure, that had ended the panic attack. Not only that, she thought with a sense of accomplishment, it had been the shortest attack she'd ever experienced.

He nodded. "I can understand that. Fear is like a prison. No one chooses to live that way. Maybe becoming a parent has something to do with your new outlook. Prospective parenthood has certainly changed how I see the world." He chuckled. "Like my views on marriage, for instance. I used to be a confirmed bachelor."

Had prospective parenthood really changed his outlook? she wondered. Or was his revised perspective merely an extension of the way he'd always felt? His reason for marrying her, to give his child a father, was based on his childhood. He'd missed growing up without a dad. She supposed his wanting to be a parent was as good a reason as any to get married. Who was to say what made a marriage work? But what happened when one of the incentives no longer applied? She'd agreed to marry Tyler for a number of reasons. One, their baby should have a father. Two, it made sense financially. Three, she would feel safe. But suddenly the last reason no longer seemed paramount. Yes, she still was afraid, but she was no longer willing to live, as Tyler had put it, in a prison of fear.

Great. She'd just gotten married yesterday, and already she was having second thoughts.

"Truce?"

Jarred from her thoughts, she looked up at his expectant face. Well, why not? They were married, and she might as well make the best of it. No one said they couldn't be friends. Besides, her other two reasons were still valid. She forced her doubts aside and answered, "Truce."

He gave her a shy smile. "You know, I never answered your question. You asked me what I was doing here."

"What *are* you doing here?" she asked tentatively.

His smile grew wide. "I decided to drop by the office and take my wife out for a night on the town. After months on the trail, Nick and I finally made the bust, and I wanted to celebrate. The perp had the decency to make his drug deal early in the evening, so after we booked him, I came right over."

"How did you get upstairs?"

"George Hammond, the night security guard, is a retired cop. He used to work for the department. We talked for a few minutes about the force. Actually, he did most of the talking, about the old days. Then, after congratulating me on our marriage—said I had great taste, by the way—he let me come up through the back stairs. He unlocked the second-floor door by remote."

"Why did you go through the store in the first place? You could have taken the outside stairwell. There's a bell. I would have heard it."

"But would you have answered? I would have sounded like an idiot, yelling at the top of my lungs through that steel door. Besides, I wanted to surprise you. Note I said surprise you, not put you in a coma. Which is why I called out your name as soon as I stepped into the corridor."

She felt her ire stirring. "Obviously you didn't call out loud enough. And why on earth would you think I'd want to be surprised? I hate surprises—didn't you learn anything in couples therapy? And even if I were inclined to like surprises, which I don't, you knew I was alone. What were you thinking, creeping up on me like that?" Some truce. He'd broken it in less than a minute. Angrily, she turned her head away.

Her gaze fell on the receipts lying on her desk, and anxiety quickly replaced anger. She had to hide them before Tyler saw them. Fact was, when it came to Walter, Tyler was the enemy. He was working for the other side.

But what if he'd already noticed the receipts? What if he'd memorized what was written on them?

Calm down, she ordered herself. He hasn't seen them. He might be able to keep a poker face with strangers, but she was his wife. Albeit, she'd been his wife for only a day, but she knew his expressions. If he'd seen the receipt for the diamonds, the look on his face would have given him away. She hadn't known who Van Damon was, but she had no doubt that Tyler would have recognized the name immediately.

"Can you get me some water?" she asked, forcing her voice to remain steady. "The cooler's just down the corridor." As soon as he stepped out of the office, she tossed the receipts into her drawer. He returned just as she was dropping her desk key back into her purse. "I'm much better now," she said, after gulping down all the water at once. "Thank you. And I'm sorry. Again. Sometimes I overreact. I'll try to watch that."

He shrugged. "Hormones," he repeated.

She looked at him and smiled. "You mentioned a night on the town. A celebration for cracking the case. Why didn't you go out with Nick? I wouldn't have minded."

"Aw, hell, I can't lie to you. This doesn't have anything to do with the drug bust. I mean, yeah, it does, but only because we finished early. The whole time I was sitting in the car, waiting for them to make the deal, I kept thinking about our wedding. Maybe it wasn't the most memorable ceremony, but marriage is a still a big step. It deserves to be celebrated in some way."

It seemed she wasn't the only one who had regrets about the way they'd handled it. "What did you have in mind?" she asked, her curiosity piqued.

"I didn't have anything in mind, exactly. I just knew I wanted to make up for last night. I tried calling you, but there was no answer. Then I remembered that you said you never answer the phone when you work late, so I thought I'd take a chance and swing by. I saw your car out front. This weekend, I'm buying you a cell phone, by the way. Not a very romantic wedding present, but a definite necessity. You'll feel a lot safer knowing that 911 is just a speed button away."

He really was a sweetheart, she thought, her heart growing warm. "If you still want to go out with your shrew of a wife, I'm game. A night on the town could be fun. I feel fine now. It was just the shock that made me woozy." She suppressed a chuckle. Here they were, a married couple, and they sounded as if they were making a date.

His gaze roamed over her, then lingered on her legs. "I see you're already dressed for the occasion," he said, his eyes shining appreciatively. "You look nice, Linda. Just like the night we—" He stopped abruptly.

"What is it?" she asked, alarmed.

His voice grew quiet. "You still haven't told me why you're dressed like that."

"What's wrong with this outfit?" she asked, tugging at the hem of her skirt. "You didn't seem to have any objection the first time you saw me in it."

"And I don't have any objection now. But you were wearing different clothes when you left this morning."

She felt her face flush. "I never realized that having a husband meant having a clothes monitor. If you must know, I went home after work. I changed my clothes and went downtown to meet, uh, Charlie. But then I remembered something I had to do at work, and I drove straight back to the office." She'd nearly blurted "Charlene," but thankfully she'd remembered the nickname the man at the bar had used. Charlene wasn't an uncommon name, but why take a chance? Tyler would know plenty about Walter's previous accountant, including the first name of Ronald Pritchard's girlfriend.

He eyed her suspiciously. "Charlie?"

"Don't get all ruffled. Charlie's a woman."

"You've never mentioned anyone named Charlie, and you still haven't told me why you changed your clothes."

He was acting like a husband who'd come home early and found his wife in bed with his best friend. Did he really think she'd gone out to meet another man? Impatience and astonishment warred inside her. Impatience won. "Contrary to what you might believe, you don't know everything about me. We might be married, but we're still strangers. You don't know everyone I know. Take Charlie, for example. What is this, anyway?" she charged on. "The third degree? What are you, my keeper?"

"Why are you being so defensive? I'm not your keeper, but in case you've forgotten, we're married. We can't go around doing our own thing without advising each other of our plans."

"The way you advised me of *your* plans? What about the way you sneaked in here? You know what I think? You didn't want to surprise me, you wanted to catch me off guard." Involuntarily, she glanced at her desk drawer and then quickly averted her gaze. "Just because we're married, don't think I'm going to let any information regarding Walter fall into your hands. On the contrary, I'm going to be more careful than ever."

"I'm not spying," he said tartly. "I admit it would be nice having my wife on my side, but trust me, I'll get Walter with or without your help, and I won't have to stoop to his methods to do it."

She shook her head. "I want to believe you, really I do, but what else can I think? You didn't come here to surprise me—no one could be that thoughtless. Sneaking around like a prowler, you nearly gave me a heart attack! So what else should I believe? That you came after me in a jealous rage? I suppose it makes sense, after the way you grilled me about the way I'm dressed. Did you think you'd find me in the arms of a lover?"

He let out an ugly snort. "You? A lover? I don't think so."

All right, so maybe he hadn't come after her in a jealous rage, but he didn't have to be insulting. "What's that supposed to mean?"

"Nothing. Forget I said anything."

"No, tell me. I want to know."

He sighed. "Linda…"

"Don't Linda me! Why is it so impossible? Am I really that repulsive?"

"You're the most beautiful woman I've ever met," he said quietly.

"Yeah, right. I think you've seen *Shrek* too many times. Either that, or you've never bothered to update your lines. Or maybe you think that just because I slept with you once, I'd be spoiled forever for any other man. Well, I have news for you, superstud. Not every woman falls in love with every man she sleeps with."

Oh, God. Had she just said what she thought she'd said? What was the matter with her? For someone who'd never been able to think of a comeback, she'd certainly come a long way. Only now, she'd gone too far. After what she'd just blurted, he probably thought she'd been with dozens of men.

"Are you?" he asked.

"Am I what?"

"In love with me."

She felt her face turn crimson. "Love? Who said anything about love?" *I* did, she realized, then dropped her gaze.

He tilted her chin with his hand. "Linda, look at me."

"No."

He eased her up from her chair. "What are you going to do?" she asked, her heart beating wildly.

"I'm going to kiss you."

"This isn't a good idea," she said nervously.

"Then say the words," he murmured, his face dangerously close to hers. "Tell me not to. Tell me you didn't like it when I kissed you on the beach. Tell me you didn't like it the night we met."

The memory of that first night unfolded like a movie in slow motion. She saw herself wearing the outfit she had on now. Saw herself sitting at the table in the lounge with Sadie. Saw herself smiling at the handsome young man who'd approached them.

Saw herself kissing him, right out in the open, after Sadie had left.

After *Sandra* had left.

"I liked it," she answered, meeting his gaze. "I liked it a lot."

With an ardency that surprised him, she threw her arms around his neck and lowered his head to hers. "Oh, I liked it just fine," she said in a throaty voice.

Her sudden transformation sent his senses reeling. What had just happened? Why the sudden melt? She must have sensed his misgiving, because she pulled away and looked directly into his eyes. "I know we got off to a bad start," she said, smiling apologetically, "but that was because we didn't know what to expect. We got married so fast. We hardly knew each other—we still don't. We're still trying to find our way."

He supposed that made sense. Sort of. "About last night—"

"Shh," she said, placing her fingers on his lips. "I know I came on a little strong. I thought you'd like it, especially after the way I'd kept you at arm's length. It was all my fault. I didn't know the rules."

"There are no rules," he said gruffly. "It's just that you took me by surprise."

She smiled demurely. "Are you saying you don't like surprises, either?"

He slipped his arms around her waist. "I'm saying I want you to be sure."

"I'm sure," she whispered. "I've never been more sure of anything. I want you, Tyler. Now. Here."

He'd been an idiot last night. How could he have told her to slow down when he, himself, had been on the verge of losing control? Well, nothing would stop them now. He'd held back these feelings too long—feelings for her, feelings he'd never experienced with anyone else. "You're so beautiful," he murmured into her hair, pulling her closer. "So incredibly beautiful. In my wildest dreams, I never believed I'd hold a woman like you in my arms."

Raw emotion took over. With an urgency he couldn't contain, he thrust her against the wall, pressing his body against hers. His mouth crashed on hers, his tongue eagerly seeking the depths of her mouth. She clasped her hands around the back of his neck, her mouth clamped to his, igniting the need in him like a brush fire. Then suddenly, he was the one against the wall, her breasts pressed against his chest, and then they were rolling, bodies revolving as if in perpetual motion—his on hers, hers on his—along the wall.

"Do it," she said in a voice that nearly drove him over the edge. "We're alone. No one's coming."

A scene from an old crime movie flashed through his head. He imagined himself in the role of the tough hero, sweeping clear the top of her desk, scooping her up in his arms, then setting her down on her desk, climbing on top of her…

"Damn computer," he muttered, swiping his hand through his hair. It took up half the desktop.

She laughed. "Come here," she said, tugging at his arm as she lowered herself to the floor. "This is why carpets were invented."

She looked so innocent, the way she sat on her knees, beckoning to him with large, expectant eyes. Yet she was his temptress, tilting her head suggestively, her mouth curling up in that tantalizing way. He didn't have to be cajoled. She was incredible, and he couldn't take his eyes off her. Couldn't believe he was finally going to make love to her again. Couldn't believe they'd have night after night of that kind of bliss.

He knelt before her, too moved to speak. He slid his hands under her halter, and she let out a sigh of pleasure. She lay back, pulling his body on top of hers. She reached under his jacket, her right hand gripping his belt, her left hand on his holster.

Her hands stopped moving.

"Get up."

He stared at her, baffled.

"Get up," she repeated.

Jeez, not again. "What's the matter?" he asked, his pulse still hammering. He pulled to a sitting position, and she did the same. Suddenly he was alarmed. Had he hurt her? For God's sake, she was pregnant. What was he thinking? He had to learn to control himself.

"Take off your jacket," she ordered.

He felt a slow tug at his mouth. Ah. So that's how she wanted to play it. Tough. The one in control. This was a continuation from last night, but tonight he had no intention of botching it.

"You got it, lady," he said, pulling off the jacket. "Is there anything else you'd like me to remove?"

She stared at him, her face pale. "That," she said, motioning to his gun. "Take it off. Please."

He removed the holster and placed it on her desk. "There. Is that better?"

"No. I can still see it. Cover it with your jacket. I don't like guns."

"You're afraid of them," he said matter-of-factly. Now that was bright. Of course she was afraid. That wasn't lust shining in her eyes; it was fear, sheer and naked. "You're right to be scared," he said carefully. "Guns are dangerous, and in the wrong hands they're disastrous. But you're married to a cop. I live with guns, and now so do you." He eased her to her feet. "I want you to touch it," he said softly. "I want you to get to know it. I want you to know what it feels like."

She pushed away his hands. "I already know what it

feels like. I already touched it. At the hotel the next morning. You were still asleep. I saw it lying on the bureau, I touched it and then I ran off. I don't like guns," she repeated.

It was fine to have a healthy fear of guns, but she was bordering on hysteria. "It helps to talk about it," he prodded gently. "Didn't you say that you don't want fear to control your life? Linda, can you tell me what happened?"

"I just told you. I touched it, and it frightened me."

"That's not what I mean. What happened to make you so scared?"

"You know what happened," she whispered. "My mother was shot."

"Touch the gun," he said, determined to get her past this. "Don't worry, the safety lock is on, and I'll help you." He took her hand in his and placed it over the weapon. "That's not so bad, is it?"

"No," she said with uncertainty. "I guess not."

"I'm going to take my hand away. When I do, tell me what you feel."

She nodded slowly. "Okay, I'm ready."

He lifted his hand. "Well?"

"It feels the same as before. Cold. A chunk of metal."

"That's exactly what it is." He picked it up, and with a flip of his finger the magazine dropped out. He pulled back the slide on top of the gun and locked it. "Now it's not loaded," he said, putting his finger in the empty chamber. "I want you to hold it."

She took it from his hands. "It's heavy."

"It's a .40 caliber semiautomatic Beretta. You bet it's heavy."

"It could go off," she said nervously. "I could kill you."

"It's not loaded, remember?"

"But what if it was? Accidents happen."

"Statistically, the chance of dying from an accidental discharge of a firearm is one in two hundred thousand. You're almost thirty times as likely to die in a car accident."

She frowned. "That's a cheerful thought."

"Look, I'm no advocate for or against gun control. All I'm saying is that guns don't go off by themselves. As I said, you're smart to have a certain amount of fear, but remember, guns have no magical power. Tell you what. Tomorrow, I'll take you to the firing range, and we'll fire off a few rounds. You'll feel more comfortable after that."

"I don't know. I'll have to think about it." She put down the weapon. "I don't know how anyone can say he's comfortable with guns."

He could sense from her tone that she was still upset. "Linda, tell me what happened. All of it."

She spoke slowly, staring at the gun. "My mother told me not to go, but I went anyway. I was tired of listening to her go on and on about how boys were bad, how they only wanted one thing. All my life I'd done exactly what she'd told me to do, but that night I didn't listen. There was this boy, Daniel. Daniel Farber. I had a huge crush on him, but until that day, he'd acted as if I didn't exist. He asked me to go with him to a party, and I said yes. I couldn't believe he liked me."

"And then?" Tyler asked gently.

"My mother was supposed to be out—she worked at a cocktail lounge downtown—but that night she was home sick. After she went to bed, I sneaked out of the house. I waited for Daniel on my front porch. I didn't tell him that my mother was home. I was afraid he'd think I was a baby, if he knew I'd had to sneak out like that."

She stopped, and Tyler waited for her to continue. He could see how difficult it was for her to talk about what had happened, and he didn't want to push her. When she started to speak again, her voice was hard. "Daniel was friends with Timothy Sands, the boy who shot my mother. They ran in a rough crowd, the same crowd that was at the party. When Daniel and I arrived, I knew right away I'd made a mistake. Some kids were chugging beer and others were doing drugs. Some were taking turns going into the bathroom in twos and threes, doing God knows what. I told Daniel to take me home, but he laughed, called me a freak. I went upstairs. I thought if I stayed hidden, I'd be all right. Sooner or later, the party would break up, and Daniel or someone else would drive me home."

The creep probably came after her. Date rape, Tyler thought, and felt a surge of rage. So help me, he vowed, even after all this time, if I get within one foot of him… He didn't know what he'd do, but he knew it wouldn't be pretty.

"Nothing happened," she said, immediately putting his mind to rest. "But I decided I didn't want to wait around and take a chance. So I left. No one even noticed. I left and walked the four miles home."

"Thank God nothing happened," Tyler said, not bothering to hide his relief. In his relatively short career, he'd come across the same scenario time and again, except that the endings had been tragically different.

"Thank God?" she repeated, blinking. "When I got

home, there were police cars everywhere. My mother had been shot in cold blood, and for what? A handful of costume jewelry and a few measly dollars. Later, people kept telling me it wasn't my fault, but the fact remains, if I hadn't gone out that night, if I'd listened to her, she'd be alive today."

He gently pulled her to him and stroked her hair. "You couldn't have known what would happen. No one could. Sands is to blame, not you. He broke into the house. He shot your mother."

Suddenly agitated, she pulled away. "I knew what was going on, don't you see? At the party, while I was waiting upstairs in a bedroom, I overheard a boy's voice coming from the hallway. I went to the door and peeked out. He was bragging to a girl about a robbery that had taken place a few houses down from mine. He described how Timothy had orchestrated the whole thing, how he'd made sure no one was at home, how he'd broken in and gotten away with more than five hundred dollars. When the girl asked where Timothy was now, the boy laughed. I should have figured out what was happening, but I didn't want to admit that I'd been used. I felt so stupid. It was all a setup, my getting invited to that party." She looked down at her hands. "I was a nerd, and I dressed like I belonged in a convent. Timothy had heard about me from some kids at school. I'd told them that my father was a foreign correspondent, and that soon he'd be coming home for good. But that wasn't all. I'd said that he'd given my mother some expensive jewelry so she wouldn't forget him. How ridiculous was that? But they'd believed me, and Timothy, apparently, had believed them. He got Daniel to invite me to the party so the house would be empty. And it would have been, if my mother had gone to work."

"Timothy is locked away for life," Tyler said. "What happened to Daniel?"

"Even with my statement, there wasn't enough evidence for an arrest. He disappeared after Timothy's trial, and that was the last I heard of him." Tears flowed freely down her cheeks. "Daniel was the first boy who ever paid any attention to me. I'd never believed that someone could like me, and until that night I'd never disobeyed my mother. When she died, part of me died, too. Time went by, and men started asking me out, but I wasn't interested. Maybe I believed I was undeserving, I don't know. I just knew that something in me was missing." She smiled shyly through her tears. "You were the first, Tyler."

She was saying she'd been a virgin that night at the hotel. A thirty-year-old virgin. Yet as inexperienced as she'd been, she'd made him feel as if no other man had ever mattered. No other man? Hell, he'd been the only man, period. It was true that not all women felt pain the first time they made love, but dammit, how could he not have known that she was a virgin?

"Let's get out of here," he said, fearing his voice would catch in his throat.

The office was no place to consummate a marriage. Their first time together as man and wife had to be special. But he didn't know when that would be. It could be tonight or sometime in the future. All he knew was that he wanted her to want him as much as he wanted her, without false bravado, without pretense. As wonderful as their first night had been, it had been based on fantasy. He wanted honesty. He wanted the real thing.

Chapter Nine

Tyler was waiting for her in the parking garage when she arrived at the apartment. He pushed the button for the elevator, and silently they entered, the tension inside so thick she swore she could see it.

"I'm a little more tired than I thought," he'd said as they left her office. "Tonight's bust was a little tricky, and it's just catching up with me now. Do you mind if we postpone our night on the town for another time?"

She wasn't surprised that he'd wanted to go straight home. Who wanted to be around a wet blanket like her?

Why was the elevator moving so slowly? The apartment was only four floors up from the basement, but at this pace it might as well have been on Mars.

She couldn't believe the things she'd told him. Couldn't believe she'd spoken about her past at all. Maybe it was the cop in him, but Tyler had a way about him that got her to open up. She wasn't sure how that made her feel. On the one hand, she didn't want to trust him. As long as he was working against Walter, she'd have to watch what she said. On the other hand, she'd liked how she'd felt in his arms, in spite of her earlier resolution not to depend on anyone to make her feel safe. She'd found herself wanting to confide in him, wanting him to reassure her that nothing bad would ever happen to her again.

She had to admit, though, reassurance wasn't all she'd craved, and safety wasn't the only thing she'd desired in his embrace. She'd tried to convince herself that the stirrings she felt weren't real, that the way she was dressed had catapulted her into a kind of alter ego. Yeah, right. Who was she kidding? Her outfit had merely helped her shed her inhibitions. She would have wanted him even if she'd been wearing a pillowcase, and she wanted him now.

But Tyler had rebuffed her twice—in their bedroom and at the office. How many times could she take his rejection? He'd once said that he wanted a real marriage; obviously his definition differed from hers.

Granted, she was the one who'd broken the mood when she'd felt the gun under his jacket. But the way he'd practically whisked her out of her office, after she'd confided in him, had been nothing short of abrupt. Before they'd left, she'd gone to the ladies' room to splash cold water on her face, and when she'd emerged he was already at the exit in the corridor, holding her coat, anxious to leave.

The elevator passed the second floor. So slow… agonizingly slow. Not wanting to meet his gaze, she stole a glance out of the corner of her eye. He was watching the floor numbers flash overhead as the elevator continued its snail-like ascent.

She didn't know what she'd been thinking, coming on to him like that, not once, but twice. She'd never been the sort of person to make the first move. Make the first move? Come on, be honest, she reprimanded herself. Until she'd met Tyler, she'd never even considered having sex. Now, the problem was, she didn't know how to proceed. Was it her aggressive behavior that had turned him off? He hadn't complained that first night at the hotel. She didn't know what she was doing wrong; it wasn't as if she had much experience to fall back on.

The number four lit up, and she stole another glimpse at him. His gaze was still locked on the overhead display as though it contained the answers to all the secrets of the universe. The elevator finally came to a stop and the doors opened, and in continued silence they headed down the corridor.

He unlocked the door to their apartment, then turned to her with a shy smile. "I hope you're not angry about the change in plans. I think this is better, anyway. We could use some quiet time alone. It's true what you said in Reverend Nelson's office. We don't really know each other at all."

She couldn't argue with that, and she knew exactly what they could do to amend the situation. She'd give it one last try; after all, it took three strikes before you were out. But she'd learned a thing or two from her last two attempts. This time, she'd be less direct.

"Aren't you forgetting something?" she asked coyly.

"You first?" he asked, moving aside so she could enter.

"Always the gentleman. But no, I'm not talking about etiquette. It's customary for the groom to carry the bride over the threshold. You didn't get a chance to do it last night."

He hesitated, then gently gathered her up into his embrace. She wrapped her arms around his neck, and... nothing. He didn't even look at her as he set her down in the entryway.

"I didn't have time to eat tonight, and I'm famished," he said. "What about you? Are you hungry? What do you say we order a pizza?" He took their coats and hung them on the rack, then plopped down on the futon. He kicked off his shoes and leaned back, resting his feet on the coffee table.

Pizza? The last thing on her mind was pepperoni and cheese. She sat next to him, regarding him closely. She couldn't deny that he looked tired, and maybe he really was hungry, in which case a meal would revitalize him. He'd need all the energy he could get if they were to finish what they'd started at the office.

"Why order out when we have a full freezer?" she asked casually. Delivery was so slow, and she'd waited long enough, thank you very much. To be precise, thirty years for her first and only time, but who was counting? "I've already eaten, but I can nuke you something. It'll save us a lot of time."

You didn't get more subtle than that. Nevertheless, she resolved, if he rebuffed her again, she'd nuke him instead.

He kissed her on the forehead. "No, I don't want you

to bother. You're tired, too, and you've had a stressful evening. We have to think about the baby."

Since when was nuking a frozen dinner stressful? "Tyler, I'm perfectly fine," she insisted, frustration setting in. She was more than fine, and she wasn't the least bit tired. She felt like a revved up engine with no place to go.

Strike three, she thought miserably.

He took out his cell phone and was about to start dialing, when suddenly it buzzed in his hand. After speaking in that cryptic cop terminology, he disconnected, frowning. "So much for a quiet evening at home. That was the precinct. Gotta go, sweetheart. There's trouble with a case." He kissed her again, this time on the cheek. "Don't wait up for me. I don't know when I'll be back." He grabbed his coat and was gone in a flash.

What had just happened? She wasn't referring to his sudden exit; as a cop's wife, she knew she'd have to get used to his being on call. She was referring to the way he'd treated her, as if she were a porcelain doll. And what were those chaste kisses all about? He'd acted as if she'd shatter if he so much as touched her.

She entered the bedroom to change into her pajamas, catching her reflection in the mirror on the door. No wonder he doesn't want me, she thought. Her outfit had "one-night stand" written all over it, and their one-night stand was long over.

Her mother's voice entered her head. *Cheap. Tawdry.*

She stripped off her clothes in front of the mirror, then let out a small derisive laugh. He thinks I'm beautiful, she thought. He must be blind. She scrutinized her naked reflection. Okay, so maybe she wasn't that bad.

Her legs were long and shapely, her waist still trim even though she was almost three months pregnant. Her firm breasts were larger and fuller, but basically it was the same body.

Yet the closer she stared, the more she became convinced that something about her was different. Maybe it was because of the way she now wore her hair, bouncing freely down her neck, framing her heart-shaped face. She held the strands back with her hand, then let them fall loosely once again. No, that wasn't it. Maybe because of her contacts? No, that wasn't it, either. She couldn't figure it out, but something about her had definitely changed.

She turned away from the mirror and slipped into her flannel pajamas. Even though it wasn't even ten o'clock, after washing up in the bathroom she climbed into bed. In no time at all she felt herself drifting off to sleep, a strange dream filling her head with fairy-tale nonsense. She saw herself locked in a chamber at the top of a castle, like Rapunzel with long, flowing hair. "I can't get to you," a man in a soldier's uniform called out, and she immediately jolted awake.

"You must have felt like a real hero, rescuing the damsel in distress," she'd told Tyler, earlier that evening in her office.

A realization washed over her, and she groaned out loud. Afraid to come near her because she was so inexperienced, he was treating her like the proverbial virgin princess. But what about that night at the hotel? How could he have forgotten that?

She turned on the lamp on the nightstand and glanced at the clock. Four o'clock in the morning. She'd been asleep longer than she'd thought. She climbed out of bed and tiptoed to the door. Worried it might creak, she opened it slowly. In the dimness, without her contacts in place, she could barely make out the living room. Her eyes adjusted to the darkness, and her gaze rested on the futon where Tyler was sleeping soundly. At least, she thought it was him. It could just as easily have been the pillows. As quietly as possible, she darted back to the dresser and groped for her glasses. She returned to her post at the door, and what she saw made her heart flip over. Wearing only his shorts, he was lying spread-eagled on the futon, the linen heaped in a pile on the floor.

She didn't know why she found the sight so endearing. Maybe because he looked so young and vulnerable. She recalled when she'd run out of the hotel scared out of her mind. Now, the memory seemed almost ludicrous. He'd been asleep then, too. He hadn't been a threat that morning, and he wasn't one now.

She wanted to snuggle close to him, wanted to feel his arms around her. She realized then what had been different about her reflection in the mirror earlier that night. She'd seen the face of a woman in love.

Darn—no, make that *damn*—she didn't want to feel this way. She'd never wanted to fall in love. "I told you it would happen one day," she imagined her best friend saying. Well, Sadie would have a good laugh now. Except, Linda thought, if it was so funny, why wasn't she laughing?

The answer to that was obvious. How could she allow herself to love a man she didn't fully trust? As long as Walter remained between them, trust would remain elusive.

And what about how Tyler felt? She especially didn't want to be in love when the feeling wasn't mutual. Or was it? The way he'd held her and looked at her were all telltale signs that even she, a woman of little experience, could read. If he wasn't in love, he was on the edge.

He'd told her he wanted a real marriage, but for some reason he couldn't seem to reconcile Lyla with Linda. "Lyla or Linda," he'd said, "a name is a just a tag. It doesn't change who you really are." Obviously, he was confused. He might be falling in love; he just couldn't decide with whom.

She turned and went back to bed, leaving the door open behind her. She'd struck out three times, but this was just the first inning. She knew what she had to do. Subtle? She planned to give the word a whole new definition.

"What's that wonderful smell?" she asked, stretching luxuriously.

"Sleeping Beauty awakes," he said, looking her over with appreciation. Damn, even in her terry cloth robe, she was delectable. The amazing part was, she had no clue as to the effect she had on him. He returned his attention to the pan sizzling on the stove. "Hope you like pancakes," he said, skillfully tossing one into the air and catching it just as deftly.

"Apparently, the tango isn't your only secret talent. You certainly are a jack-of-all-trades. Can I do anything to help?"

He served her a generous helping. "Yes. You can eat. You have to keep up your strength. I have a full day planned for us. First, a visit to the wireless phone store.

Then, on to the shooting range. After that, I thought we'd go shopping. The apartment could use your feminine touch. And, of course, we'll need baby things, too." He regarded her carefully. "Unless you have any objections. We don't have to do anything, if you don't want to. We're married. We make the decisions together."

She sat down at the table. "I'm okay with all the shopping, but I'm not so sure about the shooting range."

"Tell you what," he said. "Once we get there, give me five minutes. After that, if you want to leave, I won't argue."

She cast him a dubious look, then sighed. "All right. Five minutes, but that's all."

He smiled to himself. His motives for helping her get over her fears weren't completely selfless. Inside that tangle of doubt and fear was a vibrant, courageous woman, and that woman was the one he wanted for his wife.

He served himself a stack of pancakes and sat down next to her. "Later, I thought we'd go out for dinner, and afterward, if you're up to it, maybe we can catch some blues at a club downtown."

"Dinner? What happened to lunch?"

"You're having it. In case you haven't noticed, it's already past noon."

She took a bite of the pancakes. "Mmm, these are good. I could get used to this."

"To serve and please. That's my motto."

She laughed. "That's 'To serve and protect,' but I don't mind the amendment."

Two hours and the purchase of one cell phone later—Does this come in different colors? Don't you have anything smaller? What do you mean we get charged for incoming calls?—they pulled into the parking lot outside the shooting range. Inside the building, he waved at a few familiar faces and reserved a lane.

"Before we shoot anything," he told her, "we need to play school."

"Ooh, that sounds like fun," she said, flirtatiously. "If I give you an apple, will you give me a bite?"

I'll give you a lot more than that, he wanted to say, but held back. There was something about a woman in tight jeans and knee-high boots that heated up his blood. Down boy, he ordered himself. You need to focus. Guns are serious business.

He led her to a row of rooms in back and unlocked a door. "These are the classrooms," he explained. "This place offers a full course in the handling of firearms."

She smiled brightly. "Okay, Teacher, ready when you are."

They entered the room and sat down at desks. "First things first," he said, picking up a small revolver from a side table. "This is a .22 caliber revolver. It's the perfect gun to start with. It's easy to handle. I'm sure you'll catch on right away."

"I have no doubt." She leaned back in her chair, crossed her legs, then uncrossed them again. "I have the best teacher in the entire school."

He wished she would stop doing that. How could he concentrate with her crossing and uncrossing her legs? "Rule number one," he said, forcing his attention back to the gun. "Always assume that the weapon is loaded." He opened the chamber and spun it around. "Empty, see?" He handed it to her. "Now it's your turn."

She took it hesitantly, then looked inside. Relief crossed her face. "Empty. Now what, Teacher?"

"Rule number one. Never point the gun at anything you don't want to destroy."

"Rule number two," she corrected, crossing her legs again. "Rule number one was always assume the gun is loaded."

"Good. You're paying attention." He wished that he could, dammit. He cleared his throat. "Rule number three. Keep your finger off the trigger until you've made the decision to shoot."

"We wouldn't want to fire prematurely," she said without batting an eyelash.

O-kay. "And lastly," he continued, choosing to ignore the remark, "always be aware of the target, especially what's around it." He then gave her a brief explanation on how the gun discharged.

"Five minutes," she said.

"Excuse me?" he repeated.

"Five minutes, you said. I believe they're up."

He put down the gun and sighed. "All right, you win. Let's go."

"Don't be silly, Teacher. I'm enjoying this. Now, where were we?"

Women. Did they all go to the same secret school to learn how to torment men, or was it a natural talent? He picked up the gun. After showing her how the mechanism was put together, he demonstrated how to load it, using blanks. "So what do you say?" he asked. "Care to fire off a few rounds? We don't have to, if you don't want to. We can leave right now."

"Just call me Annie Oakley."

For a brief moment he saw the old fear in her eyes, but she quickly recovered. He had to give her credit. She was determined to go through with this.

He handed her protective glasses and earplugs. "Safety gear," he explained as they headed toward the firing lane. "Gun blasts are pretty loud. You'll still be able to hear me, though, with these plugs in place."

"I understand the reason for the earplugs, but why the goggles?"

"Sometimes you get a backlash of sparks." He looked at her face for a reaction, but saw nothing. She was determined to prove how tough she was.

He attached a paper target to a wire and reeled it out in front. He loaded the gun, this time with live ammunition, then placed it beside the open window that looked out onto the range. "Stand with your right foot slightly ahead of your left. Place your weight on the balls of your feet."

"Like this?" she asked, leaning backward.

"The balls of your feet, not the heels." Standing behind her, he placed his hands on her waist and gently pushed her forward. "There you go."

"Do you do this for all your students?" she asked, looking back.

"You're the first person I ever taught," he admitted. "But maybe I should look into this as a second career. It seems to have some definite perks."

"Now what, Teacher?"

"Pick up the gun with your right hand. Pretend you're shaking hands with someone you want to impress. Keep your trigger finger extended straight along the side and lock your thumb down to tighten your grip. There. That's it."

"Is the safety lock on?" she asked, her voice becoming tremulous.

"Yup, safe and snug." He lifted her left hand and placed it in position next to her right hand. "See that switch? When you're ready, you'll flip it down to undo the lock. But before you do that, let's work on your aim." He gestured to the human outline on the target. "Keep your left thumb over your right, and hold the gun steady. Focus on the center ring."

"Is that supposed to be my attacker? Where's his nose? Couldn't they make something more realistic?"

He rolled his eyes. "This isn't art school, Linda." He explained how to align the gun with the target, and how to gently squeeze the trigger. "Ready?"

She took a deep breath, then exhaled. "Ready." She released the lock, took aim and fired. "Wow! Did you see that? It was like the Fourth of July! Did I get him?"

"No, but you weren't too far off."

She leaned out the window. "How far off? I don't see any holes in the target."

"Uh, about two feet away."

"Oh. That's not good, is it?"

"Here, let me help you." From behind, he placed his arms around her. He cupped his hands over hers, and together they raised the gun and took aim. "Steady now," he said, feeling a mite unbalanced himself. His chest pressing against her back, he could feel the rise and fall of her breath as she slowly squeezed the trigger.

"How did I do this time?" she asked, looking back at him over her shoulder.

"Better. You hit the target. But the idea is to shoot for the guy's chest, not his feet."

She turned around and gave him a coy look. "You'd better show me again. I don't think I understand exactly what I should be doing."

That makes two of us, he thought. Why couldn't he keep from touching her? "Let's try it again," he said, pretending to study the target. She faced forward, and once again he wrapped her in his arms.

"Tighter," she said. "I need all the support I can get."

So do I, he thought, taking in the scent of her hair. Standing near her in the close confines of the lane was scrambling his senses. He held her tighter. "Ready?"

"Ready when you are." She released the catch and fired, then put down the gun. "How did I do this time, Teacher?" she asked, still facing forward.

His hands dropped to her waist, his body still pressed against hers. "Much better."

"I think I have the general idea," she said, moving his hands slowly down to her hips. "You don't have to aim for me, but if you could hold me like this, it'll help keep me steady." She picked up the gun and aimed. This time, she was the one to ask, "Ready?"

Oh, he was ready, all right.

"Bull's-eye!" she sang out after the gun had exploded.

Bull's-eye? He peered at the outline. She'd nailed the poor guy right in the crotch. Tyler recoiled, as if he was the one who'd been shot. "Lesson's over. Time to go."

"Just when I was getting all worked up," she said, reluctantly handing him the gun.

Someone was getting all worked up, but it sure as hell wasn't her. "Are you saying you want to stay longer?"

"I thought I'd try something with a little more power. I'm just getting started."

This was the woman with the deadly fear of guns? "Wait here." He returned shortly with a larger revolver. "This is a .38 special. It's powerful enough to win a gunfight, but its kick is mild enough for even a woman to handle."

She raised a brow. "Even a woman?"

He shook his head. Give a female a weapon, and suddenly she's a feminist. "Wrong word choice," he muttered. "I meant, amateur."

"But not for long," she said smugly. "I'm a quick study, in case you didn't know."

She was amazing. Not only had she conquered her fear, she'd proved to be a reasonably good shot. He leaned against the wall and folded his arms across his chest. "I didn't know, but I'm learning, sweetheart. You'll find I'm a quick study, too."

"I'm a little tired," she said six rounds of ammunition later. "I'd like to skip the rest of the shopping, if that's okay. Why don't we go back to the apartment? I could use a short nap. It's too early for dinner, anyway."

"We can skip dinner," he said, suddenly worried. "I shouldn't have planned such a full day. I don't want you overdoing it."

"I'll be fine," she assured him. "Besides, you promised me a night out on the town."

He had to admit, he didn't want to cancel their dinner plans. He'd made reservations at a new Italian bistro downtown. It was small and cozy, the perfect prelude to intimacy. Even though he was filled with desire for her, he was determined to wait until the time was right before they consummated their marriage. Intimacy wasn't just about two bodies groping in the dark. It was about getting to know each other, about learning what made the other person happy.

But most important, it was about honesty. If they wanted their marriage to work, they'd have to talk frankly and openly about the issue that threatened to destroy it. They'd have to talk about Walter. A quiet dinner in a neutral setting would help set the stage.

"I made reservations for eight. Will that give you enough time?"

She smiled. "It's perfect. And Tyler? Thank you. I don't see myself ever packing a piece, as they say on TV, but at least now I won't break into a cold sweat every time I hear the word *gun*."

"No problem," he said, a warm feeling flowing through him. Step one in Operation Linda had been a success. Next, step two, an intimate dinner with his wife.

She brushed her lips along his cheek. He knew it was meant to be merely a simple affectionate gesture, but the feel of her mouth on his skin sent his pulse into overdrive.

Step two? His brain might still be in the planning stage, but the rest of his body was soaring ahead.

He was on the futon watching a video, when his cell phone buzzed. "Jeez, not again," he grumbled. These days, it seemed to be raining criminals. "Carlton," he grumbled into the phone, expecting to hear either Nick's or the captain's voice on the other end.

"Tyler, can you come in here, please? I seem to be having a small problem."

Linda? Calling him from the bedroom? Problem?

The baby. Something was wrong. He rushed into the bedroom. "What's the matter?" he asked, anxiety knotting inside him.

She was lying in bed on her side. Drawn up over her shoulder, the blanket was slightly bunched lower where her hands peeked out, as she played with the buttons on the cell phone. "I was testing the phone, and I was wondering what this little thingamajig is."

Relief flooded through him, and then irritation took over. "You called me from the bedroom for that? Jeez, Linda, I thought something had happened."

"Don't be ridiculous. If something had happened, I would have yelled for you." She rolled onto her back and sat up, the blanket dropping to reveal a generous expanse of cleavage. With one hand she clutched the fabric to keep it from falling lower; with her other hand she passed him the phone. "So, can you?"

"Can I what?" he asked, memory filling in what the blanket covered.

"Take a look at the phone, silly. Tyler, what is it? Why are you looking at me that way?"

Why was he looking at her that way? "You're... naked," he said, barely getting the words out of his mouth.

"Well, of course I am. I didn't want to put on my pj's. It's not nighttime, for heaven's sake."

He didn't understand the logic in that, but at the moment nothing would have made much sense. The temperature in the room had escalated to heat-wave proportions, and he suddenly had trouble breathing.

She pulled the blanket up to her chin. "I've embarrassed you. I'm sorry. But it's not as if I'm not covered up. Besides, you've seen me in the buff before. If something slips out from under the blanket, so what?"

If something slips out? Now why did she have to go and say that? He had visions of her body slipping out, bit by bit. First one long, graceful leg, then the curvaceous turn of a hip, followed by a creamy, white shoulder, culminating in the display of what he'd already been given a sneak preview. He'd told her earlier that sometimes he forgot he wasn't a superhero. At the moment, he'd trade in his shield for X-ray vision in a heartbeat.

"But if it makes you uncomfortable," she continued in a maddening matter-of-fact voice, "I'll put something on. Would you mind handing me my robe? It's on the armchair."

He supposed that after he gave her the robe, she'd ask him to turn around while she dressed. Holy Moses, hadn't she heard about the power of suggestion? How could anyone be so cruel?

Cruel—or wily? He grinned. "You don't want your robe," he stated, matching her businesslike tone.

"True, it is a little warm under the blanket—"

"And you don't have a problem with the cell phone."

"Well, actually, that little button—"

"No, the problem isn't with the phone," he said, setting it down on the nightstand, "although we do have a problem with communication."

"How so?" she asked, flashing innocent eyes.

"I don't understand why I'm fully dressed while you're in your birthday suit."

"I've been wondering the same thing," she said demurely. "That's why I called you in the first place. As a matter of fact, I think I'd much rather stay home this evening, unless, of course, you have any objections. We're married. We make all the decisions together."

"The clothing dilemma is easily remedied," he said, undoing the buttons on his shirt, "and all objections have been overruled." He glanced at the phone and then picked it up.

"I thought you said there was no problem," she said, looking at him quizzically.

He turned off the buzzer. "Not anymore."

So much for their quiet, intimate dinner in a neutral zone. His reasons for wanting it had suddenly fallen away. Or so he told himself.

He set the phone back down and then pulled off his shirt. He reached for the blanket. Tomorrow. Tomorrow, they'd deal with the rest of it.

Chapter Ten

How could he tell her what he felt? He wanted to look at her, study her, memorize every detail. The way her long shimmering hair splayed across the pillow like an exotic fan. The way her breasts gently rose and fell with every breath she took. The way her eyes bathed him with promise and desire.

He felt his throat constrict. He'd waited a long time to be with her like this again, and he had no intention of rushing.

Naked, he climbed into bed and lay on his side next to her, propping himself up on his elbow. "So beautiful," he whispered, caressing the curves of her body.

She rolled onto her side, facing him. He fingered the medallion lying in the valley between her breasts—the medallion he'd given her on the night they'd met—and his heart turned over. He'd wanted her to have something to remember him by, not knowing he'd be leaving her with something that would tie them together forever.

The baby was their first miracle. The second was that they were now husband and wife.

Brushing his lips against hers, he leaned in close. Weaving a wavy path with the tip of his tongue, he inched his mouth lower, stopping long enough to taste one nipple, and then the other, before continuing slowly down to her belly.

She stiffened, only slightly, but he sensed her unease and raised his head. "You can stop me anytime," he said gently. "I don't want you to feel uncomfortable in any way."

"No, I don't want you to stop. It's just that I never...I don't know the rules."

He grazed her fingers with his lips. "Just let yourself feel. There are no rules."

"No rules. That's what you said yesterday." She gave him a shy smile, then pulled his head to hers.

It was all the invitation he needed.

Several long kisses later, he carefully pulled away to plant his lips over her eyes, her chin, her throat. She felt as if she were melting. Slowly he continued his descent, exploring every inch of her along the way, as though memorizing her with his fingers and his mouth.

He raised his eyes and she met his gaze. Brushing his lips across the swell of her belly, he maneuvered her legs over his shoulders. After moistening his fingers with his mouth, he slipped them inside her, then lowered his head. A thrill ran through her.

She closed her eyes and sighed, but just when she was about to abandon herself to these new sensations, he stopped. Her breath came in gasps as he stroked her thighs with his tongue, teasing her gently. She let out an involuntary moan, and he quickly returned to the object of her pleasure, sucking gently while pressing his fingers inside her.

This was a new experience for her, but she felt just like she had that night at the hotel—no hesitation, no holding back. "You realize," she said throatily, "if you stop again, I'll have to kill you." She pushed down on his shoulders, pulling him closer still. Arching forward, she abandoned herself to him completely as a series of shuddering spasms took over her body.

When her breathing returned to normal, he rolled over to lie next to her, folding her into his embrace. She snuggled against him, flushed with the warmth of having been loved. "Not that I'm complaining," she murmured, "but I'm a little confused. I thought I was supposed to be seducing you."

"Sweetheart," he said, pulling her on top of him, "the night is still young. And like I said, there are no rules."

She grabbed his head with both hands and firmly planted her mouth on his. Is this really me? she wondered, amazed. Can I be this way without the costumes, without the pretense? Why not? She wasn't the same woman she'd been three months ago. Hell, she wasn't the same woman she'd been yesterday. She remembered her initial fear when she'd picked up the gun. It hadn't been easy, but she'd done it. She'd had to prove to him she could. Had to prove it to herself.

These days, it seemed she was proving a lot of things, not that making love with Tyler required much effort.

"Just the night?" she teased. "Don't you mean the entire weekend? I can tell you're a man who likes to take his time."

Not that she minded. She'd liked the way he'd adored her with his eyes, the way his languid tongue had caressed her, the way she'd responded with a powerful climax, and now she intended to return the favor. She lowered her head, but apparently he had other ideas. Gripping her waist, he pulled her to a kneeling position above him, the tip of his arousal pushing against her. He eased himself inside her, then withdrew and entered her again, then again and once more, leaving her gasping until finally he pulled her down against him, sheathing himself inside her.

They rocked in perfect unison, lazily and steadily. Heat spread throughout her body, and gradually she increased the pace. At the hotel he'd been on top of her, and she'd liked the feel of his weight. But she liked this, too, maybe even better. She liked being in control. From the look on his face, she could tell he liked it, too.

They moved together in an easy, steady rhythm. Her breasts, fuller and more tender because of the pregnancy, tingled under his careful touch. If he so much as breathed, she felt a throb inside her, and with each thrust he made, she felt herself quiver.

He sat up, and she wrapped her legs around him. She didn't mind relinquishing control. They were equal now, shoulder-to-shoulder, face-to-face. She met his gaze, and in his eyes she saw her own need. Under his frank regard, she felt her face glowing.

He lowered his lips to her throat, and she moaned. Or was the moan coming from him? She couldn't be sure. But it didn't matter. They were like one, moving together in a steady, fluid motion. When he nuzzled his mouth between her breasts, this time she was certain that the moan came from her.

Clutching his arms, she pushed against his feverish body, their pace increasing as his thrusts grew harder. He reached below to touch her at the same time that she reached down to touch him, their fingers probing, feeling the wetness.

"Don't stop," she murmured. He didn't. He moved with long, steady thrusts, faster and harder, hips moving, until finally he released his stream of passion, leaving them both breathless.

She snuggled close to him, and he wrapped her in his arms. "Off the scale," he said, grinning.

"You weren't so bad yourself, Teacher," she said, laughing. "If I'd known sex could be this good, I never would have taken up baking."

He reached over and caressed the slight swell of her abdomen. "I hope this is okay for the baby," he said, suddenly looking anxious.

"Physically, there's no problem. As for the rest, I'm sure our child has far better things to do than be a voyeur."

He looked at her with amusement. "Oh, yeah? Like what?"

"Like lie in there all curled up, thinking about how wonderful his or her life is going to be." She grew thoughtful. "Tyler, do you think babies get to choose their parents?"

"If that's true, I must have been asleep when I was given the choice. Either that, or I really messed up."

She traced little circles on his chest. "How can you say that? You loved your mother, didn't you? And the bottom line is, if you'd had different parents, you wouldn't be the person you are today."

He frowned. "And what's so special about that? I'm just an ordinary Joe trying to get by in the world."

"You're not ordinary, Tyler. You're a remarkable person. You have more integrity than anyone I've ever known, and you have the courage to act on your beliefs."

He let out a scornful laugh. "I think you're confusing courage with revenge."

"You can't fool me, Tyler Carlton. I see through your facade."

"Oh, yeah? And what facade is that?"

"You're not as broken as you think you are. If you were, you wouldn't have the capacity to make me so happy."

"You're one to talk about a facade. On the outside, you come across all business. But the truth is out, Mrs. Carlton—you're really a warm, caring person."

"And sexy," she reminded him, sliding her hand across his abdomen. "Or have you forgotten Lyla already? I think she's getting a little lonely."

"So demanding," he teased. "You're getting a little bossy in your new role of mistress of the domain."

Mistress of the domain. She liked the way that sounded. "Complaining already, my lord?" She moved her hands down to his groin and, immensely pleased with herself, felt him grow hard in her hands.

"Do I sound like I'm complaining?" He pulled her back on top of him. "Thomas at your command, my lady."

Linda was humming when she arrived at work Monday morning. She was sure everyone knew how she'd spent the weekend, sure it was written all over her face. But she didn't care. She was a woman in love, and she wanted the whole world to know.

She looked at the stack of papers on her desk and sighed. How could she focus on work when she couldn't stop thinking of him? How could she concentrate when every thought brought a shiver of pleasure?

Enough daydreaming, she told herself. Time to return to earth. She unlocked her desk and opened the drawer. And stared. Something was different. Something was wrong. Her memo pad was upside down, her tray of pens shoved to the back.

The receipts, she thought with panic.

They were gone.

"Do you have a moment, Linda?" Walter asked, suddenly at her side. Startled, she looked up at him. It was as if he'd materialized out of thin air.

Walter. Walter had keys to everything. "Of course," she said, trying to keep her voice from betraying her.

He closed the door behind him. "Are you almost done checking the records? The IRS is sending someone over on Wednesday. How do we stand?"

"There's nothing to worry about," she mumbled, feeling the blood rush to her cheeks. Damn blushing. Her face would always be a dead giveaway.

"Good." He paused. "You're a good girl, Linda. I can trust you."

She felt as if her face were on fire. Why did he always have to say that? He patted her on the shoulder and turned to leave. She drew in a breath. "Walter, wait." She couldn't just let him walk out. She had to know if he'd taken the receipts. "What can you tell me about Ronald Pritchard?" she asked, her heart pounding in her ears.

His looked at her with suspicion. "Why do you want to know?"

"There were a few entries in the ledgers I couldn't reconcile. I thought maybe the previous accountant might have filed information somewhere else, and that maybe you, uh, forgot to mention it." Now that was obvious, she thought, dismayed. She wished he would stop looking at her like that.

He shrugged. "What can I tell you? Ronald Pritchard was incompetent. He was a compulsive gambler who let his addiction control his life. I tried to help him. At first, I even paid off his debts. I tried to get him into therapy, but he wouldn't go. Even after I discovered he was involved in some sort of illegal operation to fund his habit, I kept him on. I didn't want to have him arrested. He'd had too many bad breaks in his life already. But five years ago, his debts got out of hand, and when I refused to cover them, he resorted to embezzling. I had to let him go."

"What sort of illegal operation?" she asked, trying to sound nonchalant.

"I don't suppose you've ever heard of Van Damon," Walter answered, just as matter-of-factly. "He's the infamous Dutch criminal who made his fortune in Africa by looting diamond mines. Apparently, Pritchard had been making deals with him behind my back, smuggling in uncut gems at a reduced price, then funneling them into the market. But Van Damon wasn't stupid. Why should he deal with small fry like Pritchard? After a while, he approached me, but, of course, I turned him down."

"I see," Linda stated. Why was Walter so willing to disclose this information?

"All this isn't classified," he said, as though reading her thoughts. "The reason I never mentioned it before is because it's ancient history, and I never thought it would come up again. But with the investigation under way, you probably should know everything. The more you're aware of, the better prepared you'll be if you're questioned." He gave her a twisted smile. "You and I both know I'm not guilty of those reprehensible crimes they're accusing me of, but if you find anything out of the ordinary in the records, I want you to come to me immediately. The authorities have it in for me—I wouldn't put it past them to embellish something that's not quite clear."

"If the truth is there, the authorities will find it," Linda said. She didn't know what else she could say without sounding suspicious.

"Will they? Some people resent the way I do things, professionally as well as personally."

"If you mean Tyler—"

He raised his hand as if to ward her off. "Let's not go there. I can tell you're happy, and I don't want to say anything to make you feel you have to choose between us. Right now, I'm talking about Robert Jackson, the prosecutor assigned to the case. He's tricky and ambitious. A conviction like this would cement his career."

"Surely you don't think he'd do anything illegal," Linda said.

"Sadly, yes," Walter answered. "Just because you work on the side of the law doesn't mean you live there. I know what I'm talking about. How do you think I got Timothy Sands arrested? Everyone has a price, Linda. It's a tough lesson to learn, but the sooner you learn it, the better off you'll be. Less disappointment that way. Fewer expectations shattered."

She felt slightly woozy. "What are you saying? That you bribed the authorities?"

"I'm saying that I did what I had to do to secure your safety. He murdered your mother. What difference does it make how he got thrown back in jail? He's where he belongs."

After Walter left her office, Linda sat back in her chair, thinking. Walter had taken a risk by going outside the law to ensure her safety. Was going outside the law so wrong when it was done in the name of justice? Somehow, she knew how Tyler would answer. He would say yes. And yet, shouldn't justice prevail? Wasn't that what Tyler believed in above all else?

Ethics aside, she couldn't ignore the fact that Walter had taken a risk for her, and immediately she was filled with guilt for thinking he had broken into her desk. But if he hadn't taken the receipts, who else could have done it?

She felt a sinking in the pit of her stomach. What about Tyler? If he believed that justice must prevail above all else, surely he wouldn't let a little indiscretion like stealing from her desk stand in his way.

She thought back to Friday night. What if he'd seen

her shove the receipts into the drawer? What if the look on her face had set off an alarm? Before leaving, she'd gone to the washroom to freshen up. She hadn't taken her purse with her. He could have easily looked inside and scooped out her keys.

Walter had said he didn't want her to feel as though she had to choose between him and Tyler, but wasn't that exactly what she had to do? Who had taken the receipts? Tyler, because he needed evidence, or Walter, because he had something to hide?

Because of what Walter had done for her, she wanted to give him the benefit of the doubt. And yet, with all her heart, she wanted to believe in Tyler.

If anyone had answers, it would be the one person, outside of Walter, who knew what the receipts meant. But Ronald was dead, and the dead couldn't speak.

An idea came to her. Tyler was working tonight. He'd never have to know what she was up to. It was time she had another talk with Charlene Butler.

Tyler sat at his desk in the precinct, trying to catch up on the mounting pile of paperwork that filled his inbox. He couldn't concentrate. The memory of the weekend was still fresh in his mind, and he was impatiently waiting for the day to end so he and his bride could resume where they'd left off. The problem was, tonight he was staking out an illegal gambling parlor and he didn't know when he'd be home. For the first time in his life, a regular nine-to-five job began to look appealing.

Something else occupied his thoughts, as well. Knowing that Mark would be at the bookstore today,

Tyler had stopped by on the way to the precinct to talk to him about a case. He leaned back in his chair, as the events of that morning unfolded in his mind…

"I have news," Brooke had chimed in, after joining him and Mark in the café. "I'm so happy, I could shout it to the world."

Mark took his wife's hand and said, "Derek got an interesting tidbit of information in the mail."

Tyler's curiosity was immediately piqued. A few months ago, Brooke's father, Derek Moss, had come forward with his stunning story, claiming he'd seen Walter throw Jeremy's body overboard on that ill-fated cruise twenty-five years ago. But Tyler knew that Derek's testimony wasn't enough to warrant an arrest; the prosecution needed more evidence. Tyler held his breath, waiting for Mark to speak again.

"Seems that Walter wasn't the only one who did a little philandering," Mark said. He immediately added, "Sorry, bud. That was callous of me."

Tyler shrugged. "You don't need to mince words. Fact is, Walter and my mother were involved. I'm evidence of that. Go on," he urged.

"No, let me tell him," Brooke said, her eyes gleaming with excitement. "Apparently, Walter's wife, Anna, was briefly involved with my father. They'd met on the cruise ship. But that's not all. Nine months later, Anna gave birth to a son, Benton. Anna gave him my father's real last name, Ross."

Tyler shot straight up in his chair. "Are you saying it's possible that Anna was with Derek when the murder took place?" One witness could be dismissed in court under the clever examination of a good lawyer, but two… "Where is this Benton guy? Can we get in touch with Anna? When did—"

"Slow down, bud," Mark said. "Derek's already talked to the D.A. You should know, however, that Jackson doesn't think anything will develop from this. But I wouldn't worry. We'll soon have Walter behind bars, regardless."

"Nothing will develop from this!" Brooke exclaimed. "Maybe not as far as the case is concerned, but you seem to have forgotten one small detail. I have a brother. I want something to develop, all right. I want to find Benton. All my life I believed I was an only child, and now I find out differently. No one can possibly understand how I feel. I can't wait to meet him."

Not understand how she felt? If anyone could empathize, Tyler was that person. He was in a similar situation, except that Brooke seemed to be handling the discovery of her father's philandering, as her husband had put it, a lot better than Tyler had handled the news that his mother had cheated.

Then again, Brooke's father hadn't been murdered.

But an attempt *had* been made on Derek's life. Tyler remembered the bullet Brooke had unwittingly taken for her father, and admiration for her climbed ten notches. In spite of everything that had happened, she saw only the plus side. She'd gained a brother in the process. And she'd found love.

It seemed that Brooke's situation was more like his than he'd originally believed, he thought now, sitting at his desk. He, too, had found love from all this. If not for Walter, he wouldn't have moved to San Francisco, and he wouldn't have met Linda.

Love. He repeated the word in his mind, as if it was a sacred oath. *Was* he in love? He wasn't sure. He did know, however, that he'd never felt this way before. Linda had reached a place in him he hadn't even known existed, as though she could see into his soul.

Oh, he was in love, all right, but the discovery didn't please him. Friendship—mixed with respect and a healthy dose of lust—was one thing, but love was something else. Love meant sharing everything in your heart, something he was loath to do. Linda had her own heartache to deal with; she didn't need his, as well.

But that wasn't the only reason he didn't want to love her. He thought about his parents. They were proof that love didn't last.

Soon after Tyler had moved to San Francisco, he'd met with Robert Jackson to review Walter's case, which had only recently been reopened. The prosecutor had shown him Jeremy's old correspondence, hoping that Tyler would find something the investigation might have missed. Much of the correspondence, however, had nothing to do with the case. It consisted of letters that Jeremy had received from Marla, Tyler's mother, written while in her last year at college before she and Jeremy were married. Reading them, Tyler had learned that his mother and the man he'd believed to be his father had once been very much in love.

Anger filled him. If they'd been so much in love, how could they have let it slip away? He might not have learned anything new regarding the case, but reading the letters had reinforced what he'd always suspected. Love was something anyone with half a brain should avoid. Look at the misery it had brought his mother.

One love letter in particular came to mind. It had described how over the summer vacation Jeremy and Marla used to watch the sunset, planning their life together, sharing secrets as they sat hand in hand in the gazebo. Something stirred in Tyler's memory, but it was something he couldn't pin down.

His thoughts returned to the investigation. One letter from Jeremy had described a box of files that contained details regarding Walter's smuggling activities. The letter had been addressed to the FBI, but because of Jeremy's untimely death, it had never been completed or sent. Its existence had raised a question. Jeremy had recently formed an alliance with Walter; if he'd become suspicious of his new partner, why had he gone on the cruise? The question had never been answered. But the question wasn't what was nagging at Tyler now. It was something on the edge of his consciousness, something he couldn't quite define.

After the accident, the Carlton estate had been searched, but nothing had been found. The letter to the FBI had stated that the box of files was in Jeremy's home office; Jeremy must have moved it just before the cruise. Either he'd feared it would fall into the wrong hands if something were to happen to him, or he'd believed that Walter planned to have the property searched while they were out at sea.

Once again, the love letter from Marla to Jeremy rose in his mind. He recalled the police report that had detailed the search of the old property. Feeling as if he'd been socked in the gut, he realized what had been eluding him. Nowhere in that report had he read anything about a gazebo.

* * *

Last week, Charlene had told her to come by at eight, so Linda figured that eight would be the best time to show up tonight. Not wanting to sit alone in the lounge any longer than she had to, Linda remained at the office until the last possible moment. This time, she didn't go home first to change her clothes. Funny, the threat of feeling inconspicuous no longer concerned her, but never would she deliberately choose to sit alone in a place whose sign read THE TAR T LOUNGE.

As before, the street in front of the lounge was empty. She pulled over to the curb, then entered the shabby establishment. The same seedy-looking man she'd seen last week was drinking at the bar.

"Look who's back," he said, giving her a lewd smile. "Did you miss me?"

Ignoring him, Linda headed to the cash register, where Charlene was reading the paper. "Hi," she said pleasantly. "I hope you don't mind my coming back."

Charlene looked up. "It's a free country. Can I get you something?"

"No, I just came back to ask you a few questions."

"Talk's cheap, sugar. I told you last week, you can't just sit around taking up space. The boss don't like it."

"Well, the boss isn't here now," Linda stated with more bravado then she felt. She pulled out a twenty and slid it across the bar. "Maybe this will help." Good grief, had she actually handed over a bribe?

Charlene pushed back the bill. "I think it's time you stopped watching those old gangster movies. Go to the table in the back and I'll be there in a minute." She glanced at the man at the end of the bar, then lowered her voice. "In case you haven't figured it out, Max over there is the owner of this firetrap. He don't like me schmoozing with the customers, and I don't need to give him an excuse for canning me."

Linda headed for the same table she'd sat at before, and Charlene arrived a few moments later, carrying two glasses. She sat next to Linda and said, "I brought us a couple of Cokes. Max don't like me drinking on the job, and I can tell you're a teetotaler. I told him I'm on break, but you better make it fast."

"I'll get right to the point. I need to find out more about Ronald."

Charlene shrugged. "What's to tell? A quarter of a century gone down the toilet. Twenty-five years I gave that man. I got nothing more to say. I don't need more trouble."

Linda took a sip of her Coke, studying Charlene over the rim of the glass. "You sound bitter."

"Bitter? Damn right I'm bitter. You'd be bitter, too, if you'd wasted the best years of your life, and all because of that low-life piece of garbage."

Linda had figured Charlene to be in her mid-forties, but the harsh lines on the woman's face made her look older. She had the appearance of someone who'd led a hard life. Linda regarded her with curiosity. "If you were so unhappy with Ronald, why didn't you leave him?"

Charlene let out an ugly snort. "Who said anything about Ronald? I'm talking about Walter Parks, the man you work for."

Linda's mouth dropped open. "Walter! What do you mean?"

"I don't mean nothing," Charlene quickly added. "Forget I said anything. I told you, I got enough trouble."

Having lived with fear so long, it was something Linda recognized easily. "You're afraid," she said softly. "But keeping quiet won't make the feeling go away. Unless you face it straight on, it'll stay with you forever."

"You're talking about Timothy Sands, the man who killed your mother."

Linda gasped. "H-how did you know?"

"You work for Walter, don't you? Ronald made it a point to learn everything he could about him. After he went into hiding, he was like an animal stalking its prey, waiting for the right time to pounce." She looked down at her hands. "'Course he never got the chance. He died last week of the cancer, just like his old man done ten years ago."

"Last week! I thought he died five years ago."

"Twenty-five years," Charlene said as though Linda hadn't spoken. "Until five years ago, we lived together. Any day now, he'd say whenever I brought up marriage. Any day he'd get his break. I knew he was a gambler when I met him, but he was doing all right. He was a lucky man, he liked to say. And he had a nice, cushy job. It was real respectable, working for that fancy jewelry store. But he was always waiting for the big break. Said a woman like me deserved the best. Said I deserved to live in style."

"Why didn't you get married?" Linda asked. "What happened?"

"What happened?" Charlene repeated, spitting out the words. "The break never came, that's what happened. And then he was gone. No phone call, no note. Nothing. When the cops came pounding at the door, I couldn't tell them anything, even if I'd wanted to. For months, I didn't hear from him. Like everyone else, I believed the papers. Thought he was dead. Then, just like that, he showed up on my doorstep. Said he still loved me, but he had to stay in hiding. He'd changed his identity—got all new papers, driver's license and everything. But he said we couldn't live together. Said it was too dangerous. So we had to sneak around."

"I guess you know from the media that Walter will probably be indicted," Linda interjected. "You'll be subpoenaed to testify."

Charlene smiled wryly. "I don't think so, sugar. What would they want with me? They questioned me five years ago, and as far as the world knows, I haven't had anything to do with Ronald since. The man I was seeing wasn't my Ronald anymore, and I got the death certificate to prove it." She peered at Linda. "Even if you go to the cops, you got no proof."

Linda thought about the receipt for the safe-deposit box, which was now missing. Even if she still had it in her possession, it proved nothing. "How long do you think it'll take before they realize that the name on the death certificate is wrong?" she asked after a long moment. "Someone, somewhere, has seen the two of you together. Sooner or later, they'll figure out that the man who died last week was Ronald." She covered Charlene's hands with her own. "You wouldn't have called me unless you wanted it all to come out in the open. You did it for Ronald. You did it because you loved him."

Charlene's laugh was scornful. "Loved him? The

man was a coward through and through. He was always afraid. Afraid that Walter would come after him. I wanted a real home. You know, a little house, a couple of kids. I wanted marriage." Her demeanor suddenly softened, and she sighed. "Yeah, I loved him, in spite of everything, in spite of all his empty promises."

"Tell me," Linda gently prodded. "Tell me everything."

Charlene took in a breath before continuing. "Ronald had a gambling problem, and because of that, he was just the person Walter needed. Walter covered his debts and kept him out of the hands of the mob—in return for Ronald's soul, I always say. Walter was doing dirty business with some creep named Van Damon, and he made Ronald keep a separate set of accounting books. I'm not proud of what I'm going to tell you, but remember, I didn't learn all the details until recently, when Ronald found out he was dying."

She picked up her glass and took a long swallow. "Five years ago, Ronald got into a hell-load of debt, and Walter wouldn't cover it. Ronald needed money real bad, so he resorted to blackmail. He told Walter he'd go to the police about the smuggling if Walter didn't give him the money. Let me tell you, Walter was mad. So mad that he put out a contract on Ronald. Ronald went underground, and I didn't hear from him for months. Like everyone else, I thought the mob had got him. But then there he was, on my doorstep."

"It must have been so hard on you," Linda said, her heart going out to the older woman. "But why didn't he go to the police?"

"He couldn't go to the cops without incriminating himself. Don't forget, he was the one who'd kept the second set of books. He'd be arrested as an accomplice. His blackmail attempt had been a bluff, a stupid scheme that cost us our future." Charlene put down her glass. "Before he went to Walter with his scheme, he stole the books and locked them in a safe-deposit box. Extra insurance, he said. When he got sick, he got even more paranoid and moved the books again. He was afraid that Walter would get his hands on the evidence. He said that Walter had ways of finding things out. Said he had connections in high places."

Her mouth quivered, and a tear rolled down her cheek. "Just look at me, blubbering like a baby." She wiped her cheeks with the back of her hand. "In the end, it wasn't Walter that got him. It was the cancer. His father died young, and so did his brothers. That last night at the county hospital, he said he wanted to set things right. Said he was sorry about everything, and that he wanted Walter to pay for what he'd done. He vowed that if he couldn't bring Walter down while he was alive, he'd do it after his death. He said I should get in touch with you, that you'd know what to do. Then he told me to search through his belongings back at the apartment and take anything I wanted. I went through everything, even his old papers. That's when I found the envelope with your name on it."

Ronald must have addressed the envelope before he decided to move the books from the safe-deposit box, Linda figured. "Where are the books now?"

"He told me he'd hidden them somewhere on the old Carlton estate. He said it would be the last place Walter would look, since it had already been searched twenty-five years ago, and now it was abandoned."

The newspapers had been full of details about the massive, run-down property. Linda didn't recall the exact address, but she remembered that it wasn't far from an antique store Sadie had once dragged her to. "Where on the estate?"

"I don't know. He was rambling in the end. I could barely make out a thing. He was talking about artichokes, can you believe? And garages, too, for some reason. Nothing he said made sense. I don't know any more than what I've told you. He died before he could tell me anything else."

Max slammed his bottle down onto the bar and both women looked up. "Break's over," Charlene said. She rose from her chair and scooted back to the bar.

Even though Linda felt sorry for Charlene, she didn't entirely trust what the woman had told her. What if Ronald had been lying? What if Walter had no idea that these books even existed? Maybe Walter's story was true. Maybe Ronald had been conducting a little business on the side. Ronald could have kept a record for himself—making it look as if the transactions were his boss's. Extra insurance, he'd told Charlene. Linda had to find those ledgers and examine them—with an accountant's eye—before the prosecution did. Even if what Walter had told her was the truth, he wouldn't stand a chance once the authorities got hold of the books.

Innocent until proven guilty. She had to give him a chance to explain. She owed him that much.

She couldn't afford to wait. Once the police spoke to Charlene, they'd be crawling all over the place like ants at a picnic. Tyler was working tonight, but his schedule changed from day to day. She didn't know when she would get another opportunity.

She'd learned from the media that the old Carlton estate was currently the object of a nasty court case. The heirs of its last owner were haggling over the proprietorship, and at present it was untenanted. She wouldn't have to worry about being seen if she went there to snoop, but where would she look first? Where on the property could the books be?

She turned off her cell phone. Tyler had told her he wouldn't be home until late, but this way, if he tried to call her, he wouldn't even have to know she'd left the office. She dropped the twenty-dollar bill onto the table and, ignoring Max again, waved at Charlene and headed for the door.

Feeling shaky, she started the car, then set off for Half Moon Bay. She couldn't believe she was doing this. In the moonlight, as she drove south along the coast, she barely glanced at the open land and farms whizzing by. She passed several roadside vegetable stands, her headlights briefly sweeping over them. But one sign in particular, lit up by a lone light on a pole, caught her attention. U-pick: Eggplant, Zucchini, Artichokes, it advertised. Something about it played on the edge of her mind.

Artichokes. Maybe Ronald hadn't been so incoherent after all.

It wasn't a garage he'd been rambling about, either, she realized. It was the carriage house, which, according to what she'd read, Jeremy Carlton had converted into a home office.

She wasn't superstitious, but the last thing she felt

like doing was traipsing around a spooky old estate, going through a dead man's office.

There's nothing to be afraid of, she reasoned. The property was abandoned. Had been for years. It wasn't as if Jeremy's—or Ronald's—ghost would suddenly manifest, demanding retribution. It wasn't as if anyone would be there at all.

Chapter Eleven

Linda pulled into the long driveway, the car's high beams illuminating the tall iron gates that barred the entrance to the property. The only other light came from the pale half-moon, casting an eerie glow across the Keep Out! sign. She ignored the warning and stepped out of the car. Crunching leaves and twigs under her low-heeled pumps, she plodded through a tangle of overgrown weeds.

She jiggled on the padlock, then peered through the gap between the gates. Behind the ivy-covered barriers, the old mansion jutted into the dimly lit sky like a medieval castle. She felt as if she'd been dropped into a gothic novel. Imagining dark foreboding walls, secret passages and torture chambers, she nearly bolted, but then, as if she could suck in courage along with air, she drew in a slow, labored breath. I didn't come all this way to be chased off by my imagination, she thought with resolve. When she turned the handle on the pedestrian door beside the gates, a loud metallic sound from the other side rattled into the silence. The clanking of chains, she realized. The door was as securely locked as the gates.

She had to get over to the other side—but how? The gates had to be at least twelve feet high, and although the adjacent wrought-iron fencing was several feet shorter, it was strung at the top with rows of barbed wire, rendering it as daunting.

A sudden snapping erupted, amplified like a shot in the night, and she jumped. Stay calm, she ordered herself. The place is abandoned. It was probably just an animal.

Was that supposed to be reassuring?

She glanced around furtively. Nothing moved. Except for a light breeze and the gurgling of a stream somewhere on the property, the night was as silent as a tomb.

Moments later, after reminding herself to breathe, she decided she couldn't leave her car where she'd parked it just outside the gates. All she needed was for someone to drive by and report it as "suspicious." She could just imagine the scene that would follow later at the police station, after Detective Tyler Carlton was called in to collect his trespassing wife. She climbed back into the car and drove a short distance until she found what she wanted. After pulling into a narrow service road, she parked next to a clump of overhanging trees that would hide her car from the main road.

She retrieved her flashlight from the glove compartment, then looked down at her purse. Large and gray and ugly, it was too cumbersome to be toting anywhere, never mind on a half-baked excursion through the underbrush. She let out a nervous giggle. What had possessed her to buy it in the first place? She tossed it onto the back seat. After removing the car key from its ring, she locked the door behind her, then attached the key to the heavy gold chain around her neck.

She gave the medallion a squeeze for good luck. St. Michael was the patron saint of policemen; maybe the protection would extend to amateur sleuths.

Shining the flashlight in front of her, she trekked along the edge of the fence, surveying the borders of the property. Chain links had replaced the wrought iron, but the fence was still topped with strings of barbed wire. About ten yards from where she'd parked, a large oak tree leaned into the yard. She stopped and stared, an idea taking hold.

No, she thought emphatically. I won't do it. I'm afraid of heights. What *aren't* you afraid of? a voice in her head tormented.

Dammit, she swore under her breath, suddenly reversing her decision. If climbing a tree was what it took to help Walter, then climb a tree she would.

Grateful she hadn't gone home to change her outfit, as she'd done the last time she'd met with Charlene, she silently blessed her practical leather pumps. After securing the flashlight under her belt, she maneuvered through the overgrown brush toward the tree. To her disappointment—and relief—the lowest branch was too high to mount.

You're not giving up now, are you? the little voice

taunted. A strategy began to gel. She could climb the links in the fence to propel herself into the tree, then climb a branch or two higher and hoist herself over the top of the wires and down the other side.

Easy as pie, she thought—easy as baking cookies, she giddily amended—as she mounted the fence. She grabbed hold of the branch and pulled herself into the tree. Now for the hard part. You can look, but not down, she told herself, as though recounting from a list of instructions. Maybe when all this is over, she'd write a book. She could call it *A Woman's Guide to Breaking into Private Property without Breaking Her Neck.*

The breeze filtered through the top boughs, and she squeezed her eyes shut, a line from an old nursery song popping into her head. *When the wind blows, the cradle will fall.* She began singing to the deaf air, then stopped abruptly. I must be crazy, she thought. Here I am facing death from a tree, and I'm singing nursery tunes.

She opened her eyes and looked at the branch above, immediately noticing a torn white cloth. Evidently, someone else had had the same idea. Hooked to a twig, the material could very well have been ripped from a person's shirt.

Ronald's?

Well, would you look at that, she mused, staring at her legs after she'd hoisted her body higher into the tree. Her rumpled black skirt had been pushed up way above her knees, exposing her thighs for all the world to see.

"So what?" she asked aloud. "Who's going to look? Owls?"

She peered into the yard. Now what? Apparently she

hadn't thought this through. Crouching on the bough, she clutched the next higher branch with one hand, retrieving her flashlight with the other. She aimed the light on the ground on the other side of fence. It was earth, she realized. Not concrete or brick. She could jump.

Or not. The drop was only seven or eight feet, but it might as well have been a hundred, and even if she did land safely, how was she supposed to get back up? She wasn't an acrobat, for heaven's sake. And she was pregnant. What if something happened to the baby? She remained motionless in the tree, chastising herself. How could she have been so thoughtless?

Well, that settled it. She'd climb back down, wait for another opportunity and come back with a ladder and wire clippers. But when she looked down again, she felt paralyzed. It was as if the tree had wrapped its boughs around her arms and legs.

Now what? she asked herself again, trying to hold back panic. Her phone, she remembered, relief flooding through her. She'd call for help. So what if she was branded That Loony Woman Who Got Stuck in a Tree? It wasn't as if she had another option.

But her phone was in her purse.

And her purse was in the car.

She gritted her teeth. You can do this, she said to herself, over and over as if reciting a mantra. She reached for a lower bough—

…will fall. The cradle will fall. The cradle…

—and slipped. As if in slow motion she tumbled down, and like Alice plunging into Wonderland, her descent seemed to go on and on. Finally, with a splat, she landed in a soft patch of mud on the other side of the fence.

She suppressed a few choice words. Grumbling to herself, she picked up her flashlight and trudged ahead. Except for a sore derriere, a few scratches along her legs and a shredded pair of panty hose, she was fine. "At least I'm in camouflage," she muttered, thinking of soldiers with mud-smeared faces. Except it wasn't her face that had been soaked with the sticky mud; it was her bottom.

Approximately twenty yards into the property, she came across the imposing four-story redbrick mansion, which, she knew, had been in the Carlton family for generations before it was sold for payment of back taxes. To the right was the old carriage house, which Jeremy had used as a garage for his vintage cars, and later, after he'd sold the collection, as his home office.

It was then she saw the gate to the woods. The lock on the latch had been broken off and was lying on the soft earthy ground. This time, she didn't hold back her language. If she'd known about the gate, all she'd had to do was lift the handle to gain entrance into the yard.

She headed toward the carriage house, carefully picking her way through the weedy terrain. The outer doors to the home office opened easily, but she quickly realized that they were merely a front. The original entrance had been kept up for decorative purposes only. Inside was a heavy oak door, and, like the iron gates in the driveway, it was padlocked.

She walked to the side of the large one-story building. The metal bars in the large window had been pried aside, the glass completely broken away. Ronald, she thought again. He'd probably used a crowbar, wearing thick gloves to avoid the shards of glass. Unlike her, he'd done his homework before attempting his break-in.

She climbed through the gaping hole, lowering herself safely to the floor. A rank smell assaulted her senses. In the direct line of the moonlight, something in the corner caught her attention. She approached it tentatively, keeping her flashlight pointed at the floor.

The carcass of a rat lay rotting in the corner.

Fighting revulsion, she swept the light across the walls and floor. Disappointment quickly replaced repugnance. Any evidence that this had been an office had been removed. The trip had been in vain.

She was about to hoist herself back onto the window ledge, when a noise outside arrested her. It was only the wind whistling in the trees, and she laughed out loud. But it was a nervous, giddy chortle. You don't believe in ghosts, she reminded herself.

She wasn't just thinking of Jeremy. This estate had history. Lineage. Here, in these decaying ruins, she could almost feel a presence, as though heritage itself were a living spirit. Four generations, she thought. What a blow it must have been to lose the property.

She tried to conjure up an image of what the carriage house might have looked like at the turn of the previous century. Horse stalls, complete with polished wood floors, concrete water troughs, cast-iron chutes and railings unfolded before her eyes. And horses, too, of course. Horses and finely crafted carriages.

Wait a minute. Would a place like this have an attic?

She pointed the flashlight at the ceiling, and was

looking for a trapdoor when another noise startled her. This time, it wasn't the wind; it was a car. Could someone see the flashlight from the road? Not wanting to take any chances, she switched it off.

Suddenly, the noise disappeared. It didn't gradually taper off, the way a car driving into the distance would sound, but ceased altogether. Whoever had been driving had cut the engine. The old Carlton estate was the only property off the road; whoever had been driving would be headed this way.

Choking back fear, she groped her way in the dark and climbed back out the window. Barely moments later, a brilliant light pierced the air just outside the fence. She stood perfectly still. The only sound above the stream and wind was the pounding of her heart.

She heard a click, and the latch lifted. She slipped behind the bushes just as the gate creaked open. Tyler. He was so close that she could practically reach out and touch him.

She waited until he'd tested the doors to the carriage house and walked around to the side—just as she'd done earlier—before she escaped through the open gate. She knew he'd hear her driving off, but unless he'd seen her parked car in the thicket, which she fervently prayed he hadn't, he'd have no idea who was racing off.

She took one last look around. Without her flashlight turned on, visibility was poor, but in the haze of the moon she could make out his outline as he walked from the carriage house to somewhere in the distance.

Hope surged inside her. He hadn't found the books. But where was he going?

She had no intention of sticking around to find out.

Right now, only one thought ran through her head. If he hadn't figured out where the books were hidden, she still had a chance to clear Walter's name.

But as she hurried to her car, something else began to plague her. Why was Tyler here? Had he been following her? She didn't know what upset her more—that she hadn't retrieved the books, which she felt certain were lying in the crawl space of the attic, or that Tyler had treated her like one of his suspects.

He'd thought he'd seen a light inside the carriage house, but when he'd aimed his flashlight into the window, he realized it had probably been just a trick of the moon. The place was empty.

He plodded through the weeds to the back of the property toward the gazebo, or rather, toward what remained of it. Boards had come loose, the roof was half gone and the paint had all but peeled away.

He questioned the wisdom of entering the structure. It looked as stable as a house of cards. But he knew the risk would be worth the reward. He couldn't imagine anything more rewarding than walking off with Jeremy's files.

He hadn't told anyone he was coming. This was something he had to do by himself. His personal vendetta, he'd coined it. It was one thing to get hold of the evidence that could put Walter away for good; uncovering it with his own hands would be like icing on a cake.

Cautiously, he climbed the three steps onto the wobbly floorboards, planks of splintered wood creaking beneath his feet. Halfway into the gazebo, he stopped. Was that a car? He stood perfectly still, straining to hear better. But all he heard was the rushing of a stream.

Moonlight filtered in through the slats in the walls, casting shadows like jail bars across the crumbling floor. He shined his flashlight into every nook and cranny, but except for the rundown condition, nothing grabbed his attention. Discouraged, he sat down on the circular bench that lined the walls.

The bench, he suddenly realized, jumping back to his feet. Didn't this type of seating often double as storage? One by one he opened the compartments, only to be disappointed. They were all empty except for the chair at the back, which housed a child's broken doll. He picked it up, the word *zombie* coming to mind. Its eyes had been pushed back into its skull, its hair stringy and tangled.

He replaced the doll into its coffin and sat back down, trying to visualize what the gazebo might have looked like years ago. In his mind he saw a two-tiered pagoda with hand-turned railings and decorative corner pieces. It must have been the focal point of the landscape, he surmised. A place to reflect. According to Jeremy's letters, it had been a meeting place for him and his bride-to-be. But how long after their marriage had it remained a place of joy? Had Tyler's mother taken her two young daughters here to play? Had the doll belonged to one of his half sisters, a gift of love from her parents?

If only walls could talk. Tyler shook his head. These rotting old boards could hardly be called walls. The rickety structure barely even stood.

He felt overwhelmed with defeat. He'd been so sure

the files were hidden somewhere in the gazebo. But there was nothing here.

He pushed a button on his watch, and the face lit up. Ten o'clock. He still had another hour before meeting Nick. The dealer they'd busted the other night was a three-time loser who'd turned informant, and they were going after the main supplier tonight. Tyler figured it would all go down around one this morning. He sighed heavily. The night ahead would be long. Maybe tomorrow he'd take the day off. In any case, he planned on sleeping late.

A smile tugged at his lips. He'd need all the rest he could get, if the past weekend was any indication of what lay in store. Maybe he could convince Linda to play hooky with him, he thought, his anticipation mounting.

He instantly sobered. He wished he could convince her to stop working for that maniac altogether.

Disheartened, he stood up and crossed the gazebo to the stairs. Under his weight, the top step cracked and broke, causing him to trip. Swearing out loud, he broke his fall with the palms of his hand, scraping them on the splintered shards. The expletives stopped, and he sat on the floor, staring at the broken step. Then, as though possessed, he pried up the pieces of wooden board and ripped them from their bed.

Funny how things worked out. After meeting with Mark at the café, if he hadn't been reflecting on how he felt about Linda, his mind wouldn't have drifted to his mother and Jeremy, and he might never have made the connection to the gazebo.

Shoved into the hollow space above the concrete floor was a metal box. He picked it up and jimmied the lock.

It would be a long night, all right. Longer than he'd planned. After the drug bust, he planned to return to the precinct and go through every one of Jeremy's files.

Linda sat at her desk, staring out the window. Last night—and all the events that had led up to it—kept replaying in her mind. She didn't want to believe that Tyler had followed her, but what else could she think? How else could she explain his turning up at the estate?

Her thoughts drifted to Daniel Farber, the boy who'd used her to gain entrance into her house. Although he hadn't pulled the trigger, she'd blamed him as much as she'd blamed Timothy for her mother's death. And she'd blamed herself. If she hadn't been so gullible, her mother might still be alive. Never again, Linda had vowed, would she allow herself to play the patsy.

First they break you and then they leave you in pieces, her mother used to say.

What if Tyler had taken the receipts from her desk? He could have made the same connection she had. He could have decided it was time to pay the ex-accountant's girlfriend a visit. If I could figure it out, Linda thought, so could a cop.

Tyler had been at least twenty minutes behind her. What if he hadn't been following her? What if he'd figured out where she was going and set out to confront her?

She recalled the folder that was missing from the archives, the file that contained transactions for the month of July twenty-five years ago. What if Tyler had taken that, too?

Not knowing was making her crazy. If he had used

her, wasn't it likely he'd been using her all along? Why should she believe otherwise? Marriage might seem like an extreme measure to get what you want, but to someone blinded by obsession, it would be only a minor inconvenience, something that could easily be amended.

Was everything between them a lie?

Stop it, she ordered herself. Here she was, ready to convict him, and she had no concrete proof. How could Tyler have taken a file from the storeroom? He hadn't even known the archives existed.

The headache she'd been fighting all day seized her with a vengeance. She closed her eyes tightly, as though she could squeeze out the pain. All this speculation is too convoluted, she thought, rubbing her temples with her fingers. If the suspicion, the sneaking around, the constant what-ifs were what being a detective was about, Tyler could have it. Numbers, now that was a different story. If people could read each other as easily as they could read numbers, the world would be a simpler place.

She thought back to their weekend and, in spite of her headache, she felt a pleasant flush. But the weekend had been about more than just sex. Somehow, she'd recaptured something she'd felt the first time they'd met. She wasn't quite sure how to describe it, but it had something to do with loving and being loved for yourself. Something to do with honesty.

Honesty? It was a strange thought for someone who'd made herself out to be someone else. She wasn't just thinking about that night at the hotel. She recalled how she'd schemed to keep Tyler from finding out about her spying and was plagued with guilt.

Just what was all this about, anyway? When it came down to it, weren't they on the same side? They both wanted to get to the truth, didn't they?

When it came down to it, this was all about trust. She had to trust the stranger she'd come to love. She had to believe that he hadn't been using her.

She had to tell him about the books.

She hadn't spoken to him since yesterday afternoon and, not wanting to wake him, she hadn't called him earlier today. Last night, before she'd arrived home, he'd left a message telling her he'd be pulling an all-nighter. He'd also said, his voice sounding tight, that he'd tried to reach her but she hadn't answered her cell.

She picked up her desk phone and punched in her home number. After the fourth ring, the machine picked up. She tried reaching him on his cell and then at the precinct. Anxiety swept through her. Had something gone wrong last night with his case? But if anything had happened to him, wouldn't someone have contacted her?

A sudden commotion outside her office jarred her to the present moment. She heard the protests of Walter's secretary, Connie, then Tyler's official voice—the one he used whenever he talked about a case—and her feet sprouted wings. The next instant, she was in the hall-way, resisting the urge to throw herself into his arms. This was an office, she reminded herself. A little deco-rum was called for. But her heart was soaring. He was safe and he was here.

Wait a minute. *Why* was he here?

Behind him was Robert Jackson, whose face she recognized from the newspapers. She glanced at the prosecutor, then back at Tyler. And then she knew. Tyler had found the books and was here to arrest Walter. It was no wonder she hadn't been able to reach him. He'd been busy putting together the puzzle—the puzzle he wouldn't have solved without the pieces he'd stolen.

So much for honesty, she thought, disgusted more with herself than with him. So much for her believing that he wasn't using her. Once again, she'd allowed herself to play the patsy. "You found the files," she managed, her voice sounding tinny in her own ears.

"You knew about them?" he asked, confusion in his eyes.

"Don't play dumb with me," she said icily. "I know what you did. I must say, it didn't take you long to make the connection to Charlene Butler. Congratulations on a job well done."

"Charlene Butler? Ronald Pritchard's girlfriend? What does she have to do with all this?"

Linda had to hand it to him, he played a convincing role. But not convincing enough. "Okay, I'll play along. If the receipts didn't lead you to the files, then what did?"

"What are you talking about? What receipts?"

"You know what I'm talking about, so you can wipe that innocent look off your face." Before she could stop herself, words of condemnation began pouring out. "I should have trusted my suspicions, when I first found out who you were. You used me for information, and you've been using me all along. It was never about me or the baby. Right from the start, it was all about vengeance. Your obsession is like poison." She let out a derisive laugh. "Tell me something, Detective. You were never even assigned to the case—who did you have to bribe so you could make the collar? Well, you got what you wanted. And here's more good news. You won't have to pretend to be the happy husband any longer. I'm letting you off the hook."

"Linda, you're not making any sense," he said, his voice strained.

She bit down on her lip. Only moments ago, she'd held back from hugging him with relief, and here she was raving in public.

But suddenly she didn't care, and she didn't care that her tears were now flowing freely for the entire world to see. She didn't care about anything except getting as far away as possible from this stranger who called himself her husband.

She ran back to her office to get her coat and purse. Walter stood outside her door, his face devoid of all expression. "I'm sorry," she whispered through her tears.

"It's all right," he said in a tired voice. "You tried. You're a good girl, Linda."

The last thing she heard as she darted down the corridor was the resounding timbre of Tyler's voice.

You have the right to remain silent...

Chapter Twelve

Tyler stared at the empty space in the closet. She'd known about his commitment to the investigation right from the start. Why was she doing this? Why now?

He'd called her on her cell phone but, as usual, she hadn't answered. Then he'd tried to reach her at Sadie's, but no one had been home. It was just as well. In his state of mind, he'd probably say something irrational, something that would alienate her even more.

He kept turning the matter over in his mind, but he was too exhausted to think clearly. It was late Tuesday afternoon, and he hadn't had any sleep since Sunday. He decided to catch a few winks and then try calling her later. He kicked off his shoes and, not bothering to change out of his clothes, fell onto the bed.

But as drained as he was, sleep wouldn't come. What

was the matter with her? Why couldn't she understand how important it was for him to see Walter behind bars?

As important as it was for her to see Walter set free, his tired mind answered.

He covered his head with his pillow, as though trying to drown out the questions that troubled him. But it was no use. His mind kept replaying the afternoon's events. He'd never forget the shock he'd seen in her face. It was a look, he knew, he'd put there himself.

"Your obsession is like poison," she'd accused.

Too wired to sleep, he went into the living room and turned on the TV, hoping it would make him drowsy. He surfed through the channels, but all he found were reality shows. My life has too much reality as it is, he thought.

He noticed the jacket to *Shrek* on the coffee table. Recalling their wedding night, he felt a pang. Her reaction to the movie had been so sweet. "Do you believe in happy endings?" she'd asked, looking at him with sad eyes.

"I believe in doing the right thing," he'd answered with self-righteousness.

The right thing? He laughed with self-reproach. Making sure that Walter paid for his crimes was the right thing—nothing would convince him otherwise—but the way he'd gone about it was reprehensible. He knew what Walter meant to Linda. At the very least, he could have warned her it was coming. Not only that, he'd made the arrest on Walter's own turf, in front of his employees. Had it been necessary to throw it in her face? The arrest could have waited. Twenty-five years had passed since the murder. What difference would another few hours have made?

Something else disturbed him, too. Slapping the

handcuffs on Walter hadn't given him the satisfaction he'd anticipated. In fact, he'd felt just plain lousy. For months, he'd dreamed of that moment, about the sweet taste of revenge, but now he just felt empty.

He leaned back on the sofa and closed his eyes. Exhaustion finally won over, and he fell asleep. But his sleep was restless and filled with bad dreams. He woke up less than two hours later, feeling more unsettled than when he'd first arrived home.

He tried calling her again on her cell. Damn, he thought, slamming down the receiver. Why didn't she answer? He called Sadie, and this time he got lucky.

Lucky? Yeah, right. The words she spoke left him feeling numb. "She refuses to talk to you."

"Can't you convince her to come to the phone?" he pleaded. "You're her best friend."

"She needs time, Tyler. Don't rush her. Trusting doesn't come easy for her. You can understand that, can't you?"

If anyone could understand, he could, he thought after he'd hung up the phone. But how much time were they talking about? A week? A month? After the death of her mother, it had taken Linda thirteen years to come out of her shell.

Imagining a future without his child, he was filled with sadness. He pictured his son taking his first steps, then pictured him starting his first day at school. He saw his daughter scoring a soccer goal, then saw her graduating from college. He imagined his life without Linda, and anger against Walter surged again. He knew that as long he allowed his hatred to control him, Walter would have the upper hand, but he didn't care. He had nothing left.

He went to the kitchen, unable to remember the last time he'd eaten. He pulled open the freezer and stared at the packages. Deciding he wasn't hungry after all, he grabbed a beer from the refrigerator. After twisting off the cap, he raised the bottle as though making a toast. "Here's to you, old man. You won, after all."

Won? What was this, a game? A war?

He slammed down the bottle in disgust, fizz oozing over the counter. Walter hadn't defeated him; Tyler had defeated himself.

Linda was right. His obsession was like poison. It had destroyed everything he'd come to realize was important. His enemy was his own hatred, and the only war he fought was with himself.

"Just like old times," Linda said as they sat at Sadie's kitchen table. "Here we are talking about life over a plate of chocolate chip cookies."

"Almost like old times," Sadie corrected. "These cookies are store-bought."

"I don't know how you survive without me doing the baking," Linda said, pouring herself another glass of milk.

Sadie shook her head, as if to convey great hardship. "I'd put an apron on Frank, but it would clash with his uniform."

"So where's our gallant pilot off to now?"

"Australia. After that, he's taking a few days off, and I get him all to myself."

Married life agrees with her, Linda thought, observing the happy flush on her friend's face. But she wasn't surprised. Even though Sadie was a successful businesswoman, marriage and family had always been a priority. "Can I ask you something?"

"Sure. Anything."

"Frank spends so much time gallivanting to exotic places. Do you ever, uh, wonder about him?"

Sadie looked confused. "Are you talking about other women?"

"I'm sorry," Linda mumbled, feeling her color rising. "That was stupid of me."

To her surprise, Sadie laughed. "You know what they say. It doesn't matter where a man gets his appetite as long as he comes home for dinner."

Linda rolled her eyes. "Tell me you're kidding."

"Who, me? When do I kid?" Sadie frowned. "You want me to explain how I know I can trust Frank, but how do you explain a feeling? It would be like trying to explain life. It just is. All I know is that I love him, and he loves me. He'd never risk what we have by doing something stupid." She took a sip from her coffee. "I know the world is full of temptations, and let's face it, my Frank is a hunk, but he always comes home to get what he's missed—me. And speaking of going home, don't you think it's time you worked things out with Tyler?"

Stunned, Linda stared at her friend. And then it dawned on her. Sadie and Frank were still newlyweds. They'd want to be alone on his days off. "I'll go to a hotel," she murmured, feeling like a fifth wheel. "I've been in the way."

"You've misunderstood me. You're welcome to stay

as long as you want. You're my best friend and I love you, but as your best friend, I have to tell you what I think, or what kind of best friend would I be? I think it's time you and Tyler made up."

Linda couldn't believe what she was hearing. Sadie knew how angry she was with Tyler. "Are you saying I should go back to him? After what he did?"

"He's been calling twice a day for a week. All I'm saying is that you should talk to him."

From the way Sadie was looking at her, Linda could tell that her friend had something more to say. "What else, Sadie?"

Sadie put down her coffee mug. "Seeing how you asked…I don't understand what he did that was so wrong."

"So wrong! He broke into my desk and then followed me to the estate. He used me, and he's been using me all along. But what makes it even worse is that he led me to believe he wanted me. He's a liar, Sadie."

Sadie raised an eyebrow. "What about you? You set out to prove Walter innocent, but you didn't tell Tyler what you were up to. In my book, withholding information is the same as lying."

"How could I have told him?" Linda protested. "He would have used anything I found against Walter."

"Look, I'm not saying you were right or wrong. All I'm saying is that not everything is cut-and-dried. You accuse Tyler of being blinded by obsession, but how are you any different?"

"I didn't steal from him. You seem to be forgetting about the receipts. He took them from my desk."

"You don't know that," Sadie countered, "and you'll never know unless you talk to him. You know what else I think? I think you're looking for an excuse to end your marriage. You never wanted to be married in the first place, but then something happened. You fell in love. Someone finally broke through your armor, and now you're frightened. Trusting a man goes against everything your mother ever taught you. You're running, Linda. You're running because you're scared out of your mind."

"So you're excusing what he did," Linda said flatly.

"You're not listening, honey." Sadie reached for her hands. "People aren't perfect. They make mistakes. All I'm saying is that you should talk to your husband. Give him a chance to explain."

Even though everything Sadie was saying made sense, Linda was reluctant to see Tyler. He'd want them to continue as if nothing had happened. Sure, now that he'd put Walter in handcuffs, he'd believe that all their troubles were behind them. Easy for him to go on, but her trust had been shattered. "He used me," she repeated, her lips trembling. "How can I forget that? How do I get past it?"

"Is this really about Tyler?" Sadie asked gently. "Or Daniel?"

"It's about trust," Linda said, trying to push her mother's voice out of her head. *Not only are men controlling, they're undependable.* "Why can't you see that?"

"I see fine, honey. It's you I'm worried about. Day in, day out, women come to the salon looking for advice. I'm no shrink, but I've learned a thing or two. A lot of the time, it's not these women I hear complaining. It's their mothers I hear. It's as if the women are puppets, and their mothers are hovering above them, pulling their strings. When your mother died, all her talk against men became your gospel. Maybe it's time you stopped letting her pull your strings. Maybe it's time you buried her words, once and for all."

Sadie wasn't saying anything Linda hadn't told herself a million times before. But it was one thing to say the words, another to believe them. Yet she wanted to believe them, wanted to believe them with all her heart. Even though Sadie was concerned about her, nothing could mask the look in her eyes. It was a look Linda envied, the look of a woman in love.

The least she could do was talk to him, she decided. Maybe their marriage could never be more than an arrangement, but for the sake of their child they had to come to an understanding. For one thing, now that Walter was behind bars, Tyler would have to agree to let go of the case. As for her, she intended to resign from her job.

She'd given the matter a lot of thought. She was resigning not because she believed Walter was guilty—she'd let a jury decide that—but for the sake of her family. If her marriage was to have any chance at all, she couldn't continue to work for the man her husband detested. How could she expect Tyler to trust her if her loyalty was divided? It would be a constant reminder of his unhappy past.

But before she spoke with Tyler, she had to see Walter. She wasn't sure who would be running the business now that he'd been arrested, but it made no difference. She was going to hand in her resignation, and she wanted to tell him herself rather than have him hear it from someone else. It was the decent thing to do.

She pulled into the parking lot outside the detention center. The only evidence that it was a jail was the tall barbed-wired fence that circled the building. Recalling the fencing on the old Carlton estate, she grimaced. Her derriere still boasted the bruises from her fall.

After entering the institution through an electronic gate, she found herself in a large square lobby. She was instructed to remove her shoes and jewelry. After passing through a metal detector, she was given back her belongings. She was led to a rectangular room, where she sat in a small booth in front of a window, waiting for Walter.

The admittance procedure had been unnerving, but nothing could have prepared her for what she saw through the glass. Behind the barrier, two guards were escorting a hunched-over, haggard-looking man to the chair facing hers. She'd heard that sometimes shock turned a person's hair white overnight, but she'd never believed it. Suppressing a gasp, she stared at Walter's face. It seemed to have lost all its vigor, as though sagging with the weight of defeat. In spite of his sixty-plus years, the man she remembered had been youthful and vibrant, but now, as he sat facing her, his shoulders slouching forward, she saw only a tired, old man.

He motioned for her to pick up the phone. Her hands were shaking so badly she could barely manage. "How are you?" she asked, trying to keep her voice steady. The question was rhetorical. He looked terrible.

He attempted a small smile. "Don't worry about me. I'm fine."

She knew differently. When she'd called Sara yesterday to check on him, Sara told had her that his health had deteriorated and that he was having chest pains. "I don't understand why they're keeping you here," Linda said, not masking her worry. "What happened to bail?"

He gave her a sour look. "With my connections, you'd think my lawyers would have been able to swing it. But apparently the judge has problems with alleged murderers running loose in the streets."

In spite of the evidence that, according to Sara, had been found on the estate, Linda still refused to believe that Walter was guilty of embezzlement. As for the murder charge, that was ludicrous. Regardless of what the world believed, she'd always known her boss to be a kind, compassionate man.

"You could no more hurt a fly than harm another person," she offered gently.

His expression softened. "What are you doing here?" he asked in a tired voice. "This is no place for a girl like you."

She summoned her resolve. No matter what she still felt for him, she had to do what was right for her family. "I came here to tell you I'm resigning."

A sadness entered his eyes. "You're doing the right thing. Your first loyalty should be to your husband. To him and my grandchild."

She looked at him with astonishment. His telling her to side with her husband was not what she had expected.

Hearing him talk about his grandchild was another surprise. "You know about the baby. How did you find out?"

"Sara was here yesterday. I tricked her into telling me. You should have told me yourself," he chastised lightly.

The Parks network, she recalled Tyler saying. And now she was part of it. "I didn't know how you'd react. I know how you feel about Tyler."

"What's important is how *you* feel. About him and about yourself."

Even now, after she'd told him she was resigning, he was thinking of her happiness. Guilt coursed through her. If he was convicted, she would never forgive herself. She lowered her gaze. "There's another reason I came to see you. I came to apologize. If it hadn't been for me, you wouldn't be here now. I left an incriminating document in my desk. Tyler found it, and it led to his discovery of the evidence."

"Are you talking about that receipt for the safe-deposit box? Tyler didn't take it, Linda. I did."

She looked up again, her pulse hammering. "What about the receipt for the gems? What about the file from the archives?"

"You've been doing your homework. Yes, I took those, too."

Although she was relieved that Tyler hadn't been the one who'd broken into her desk, the last thing she wanted to hear was that the man she'd respected all these years was an embezzler. "But why?" she asked, afraid of what he might say. If he was innocent, why would he act as if he had something to hide?

He gave her a half smile. "You've always put me on a pedestal, Linda. You've always been too trusting."

She thought about how she'd hidden her actions from Tyler and nearly laughed out loud. Trusting? Her? Well, maybe where Walter was concerned, she conceded. Even now, she wanted to believe that he was innocent; even now, after he'd confessed to her that he was guilty.

But guilty of what? The last time she checked, taking papers from an employee's desk wasn't a capital crime.

He shouldn't have taken them, but she could understand why he'd done it. Worried that the prosecution would twist anything they might find against him, he might have torn through the office, looking for red herrings. She felt hurt that he hadn't trusted her enough to confide in her, but once again, she understood. She was married to his enemy. A definite conflict of interest, she thought wryly.

She met his gaze. "I didn't put you on a pedestal, I admired you. There's a difference. And yes, I trusted you. I still do. You've always been there for me, and I won't let you down now." She felt another pang of guilt. Quitting the firm could hardly be considered an act of faith.

To her shock, his laugh was scornful. "Let me down? You've been letting me down since day one. Let me tell you something, missy. If you hadn't told me you were quitting, I would have fired you. With me trying to run things from behind bars, this company will need an accountant with a lot more savvy, something you've never acquired."

His words startled her, but then she realized what he was doing, and her heart went out to him. This was his way of setting her free without guilt or regret. "You don't have to protect me, Walter. I'm not a little girl."

"In that case," he said dryly, "big girls deserve to be told the truth. What would you say if I told you I wasn't responsible for getting Sands reincarcerated? He managed that all on his own, but I saw it as a way to secure your loyalty."

Her breath caught in her throat. He's doing this to release you, she reminded herself. But even if what he said was true, she realized, it wouldn't matter. That segment of her life—Daniel, Timothy, her mother's death—was behind her, as was her career at Parks Fine Jewelry.

He must have been so lonely, she thought, regarding him with empathy. If anyone had known loneliness, she had. "You've been good to me, Walter. For whatever reason, you hired a young, inexperienced accountant and gave her a chance. You helped me rebuild my life, and for that I'm grateful. I only wish there was something I could do in return."

Maybe there *was* something. She was surprised she hadn't thought of it earlier. "Exactly what evidence was found?" she asked, her excitement mounting. If Tyler hadn't taken the receipts, how could he have made the connection to the books?

"Jeremy kept files," Walter growled. "Apparently he'd been plotting against me for a while, hoping to get me indicted for smuggling and embezzlement."

Three things occurred to her at once. One. The books hadn't been discovered. Tyler had found something else that night, something else to warrant the arrest. Two. Tyler might not have been tailing her. He could have been there of his own accord, following up on a tip regarding Jeremy's files. Three. Without the accounting ledgers to back up the evidence, how conclusive could Jeremy's files be?

Was Walter guilty? She didn't know. All she knew was that she had to give him one last chance. It was the least she could do for the man who'd given her a fresh start. "I know that your previous accountant tried to blackmail you with a second set of books. Tell me they don't exist. Tell me they were a bluff, a pack of lies fabricated by a vindictive imagination."

His mouth twisted into a cynical smile. "All this time, I thought Jeremy would be my nemesis. When his son—*my* son—first appeared in my office, I was sure the time had come. But it turns out it's going to be that bastard Pritchard who finally nails me on that embezzlement charge."

"Tell me about the books," she urged. Her voice fell to a whisper. "I don't know what to do."

Tell me you're innocent, she silently implored. If the books exist, tell me they're a fraud. Tell me to forget I ever heard of them.

He smiled at her sadly. "You're a good girl, Linda. You'll do the right thing."

His answer left her feeling vaguely uncomfortable. Was he telling her he was guilty of the embezzlement charge, or was he saying something else? What if he figured he had nothing to lose by telling her to go to the authorities? With or without her help, sooner or later the books would be discovered.

He knew she'd be subpoenaed. Was this a last attempt to secure her loyalty? An attempt to ensure she wouldn't denounce his integrity on the stand? He'd need all the character references he could get. She suspected that without her he might not have any.

Despite the warmth of her coat, she shivered. Was this about the embezzlement charge, or was this about murder?

Tyler sat on the futon, staring at the Picasso on the wall. Linda had told him that in this style of art, it was as if the painter took everything apart and then rebuilt it. Tyler sighed. He still didn't get it. If it ain't broke, don't fix it.

Things aren't always what they appear to be, he remembered Linda saying.

When he heard the key in the lock, his first thought was that she'd returned for more of her belongings. But when she entered and he saw the look in her eyes, hope ran through him. "We need to talk," she said, and his heart soared.

She hung up her coat, then went to the window and pulled up the shades. "Why is it so dark in here?" She gave him a hard stare. "You look terrible. Did you lose your razor? And when was the last time you ate?" She turned on her heel and headed toward the kitchen.

"Linda, slow down," he said. "You said we need to talk."

"After a nice home-cooked meal," she answered, sticking her head in the freezer. "A home-cooked frozen meal," she corrected. She turned to him and smiled. "Then later, how about some fresh-baked cookies? I can make up a batch in a jiffy." She stared at the pile of dishes in the sink. "After I get this cleaned up, that is."

"Sorry about the mess," he mumbled, trying to figure out a way he could sneak into the bedroom and pick up a week's worth of laundry from the floor without her noticing.

She assumed her schoolmarm pose. "It's you I'm worried about. A person can't live this way. It's not healthy." She spun around and turned on the faucet.

He placed his hands on her shoulders. "Linda, I'm sorry." He wasn't talking about dishes, and from the way her muscles relaxed under his touch, he could tell she understood.

She rinsed off a plate and put it into the dishwasher. "I'm the one who should be sorry," she said lightly, as though they were talking about the price of detergent and not their marriage. "I shouldn't have run away from you."

He shut off the water and turned her around. "No, you were right. I was obsessed. I let myself become blinded to everything else, including how you felt about Walter. If it takes me the rest of my life, I intend to make it up to you. If you'll let me."

"No, I was the one who was wrong. Seems I've been wrong about a lot of things. Living with fear will do that, I suppose. Makes it hard to trust people. Sometimes it makes you trust the wrong people. But I want you to know that's all over. I'm not afraid anymore. I'm a lot stronger than I thought I was." She gave him a tentative smile. "Not even the thought of living on my own frightens me."

His heart fell. She'd come to tell him she wasn't coming back. "I've always known you were strong," he said, trying to keep his voice from catching, "but you don't have to prove it by living on your own."

"You don't understand. I was afraid of everything, but more than anything, I was afraid of letting down my guard. Now the only one thing that frightens me is the thought of not being married to you."

He rested his hand on her cheek. "That's not going to happen."

"No, it's not," she answered, her eyes smiling softly. "But it took me a while to realize you weren't the big bad monster I'd made you out to be. I kept fighting you, pushing you away. I used Walter as the wedge, insisting that he was innocent. But he's guilty, Tyler, just as you always said he was."

"He manipulated you. It wasn't your fault."

"I allowed it to happen. I was so afraid."

"Of being alone?"

"Of falling in love in with you." She lowered her gaze. "I hope it's not too late. I hope you can forgive me."

"If anyone needs forgiving, it's me," he said. "I allowed my vendetta against Walter to control me, and somewhere along the way I lost sight of what was important. I love you, Linda. I've loved you since the first time I saw you." He smiled with the memory. "Your hair kept falling in your eyes, and you kept pushing it away. But then you looked at me, and it was that look that pushed me over the edge. I felt I knew you. Felt as if I'd finally come home." He smoothed away a few errant strands of her hair, and she looked up at him. "I want you to know," he continued, "now that Walter has been arrested, I'm taking myself off the case. Not that I was officially on it, and for good reason. Family members aren't exactly objective." He took her hands in his. "Case in point."

She shook her head. "You've come this far. You have to see it through. No matter how you look at it, what Walter did was wrong. You might have been seeking revenge, but you also wanted justice. How could you not? It's what you do, Tyler. Serve and protect, remember? It's part of who you are, who I fell in love with."

He sighed heavily. "All this is academic. Robert Jackson doesn't think there's enough evidence to get a conviction. He got a warrant to search his house but came up empty-handed."

"I'm not surprised. I remember back in August when he'd filed something into his safe. It struck me as odd that it was practically empty. Now I realize that he'd been disposing of evidence."

"He was thorough," Tyler added grimly.

"But not thorough enough." She gave him a self-satisfied grin. "Unless I'm mistaken, you have the evidence you need. Ronald Pritchard might have kept a second set of books."

"I know," Tyler answered. The question was, how did she? Not that anything she'd say would surprise him. Which was something he loved about her. He repressed a chuckle. Life with Linda might be a lot of things, but one thing he knew—it would never be dull.

Her mouth dropped open. "You know?"

"I know about Ronald Pritchard's blackmail threat.

His girlfriend let something slip years ago, and it was in the report. But the police believed it was just a bluff."

"There's one way to find out," Linda said excitedly. "Let's go to your family's old estate. Charlene Butler contacted me, and from what she said, I figured out that the books are in the attic of the carriage house. At least, I think they are. I didn't have time to go up there."

Understanding set in, and he laughed out loud. "So it was you I saw at the estate. I thought I'd seen something in the carriage house, but I'd chalked it up to my imagination."

"You're not angry?" she asked, her voice unsure.

"You never cease to amaze me," he said, gathering her in his arms. "If you ever decide to give up accounting, you can always become a P.I. We'll be like David and Maddie in that old show, *Moonlighting.* Or Scully and Mulder in *The X-Files.* Or—"

"Okay, I get the idea," she said, grinning. She gave him a mischievous look. "The thing is, I've never seen *The X-Files.* Who do I get to play, Scully or Mulder? Maybe you'd rather I just be Lyla?"

"Not that I minded Lyla," he said, pulling her closer, "but I'd rather be with the woman I married. Turns out she's a lot feistier than Lyla ever was."

"You mean Linda, that boring accountant?" she teased. Suddenly, she looked up at him, her eyes somber. "I did give up accounting, by the way. Well, maybe not forever, but I'm no longer working for Walter."

He knew how difficult it must have been for her to let go, and he felt his heart swell—with love, because she'd done it for him; with pride, because she'd done it for herself. "You did it for us," he said softly. "You did it for our future."

"So much has happened in such a short time," she said, the somber expression still in her eyes. "Do you think we've moved too fast?"

"Sometimes it happens that way. Sometimes you know right from the start."

She nodded. "Those were Sara's words."

"And they happen to be true. I love you, Linda. I loved you the first night we met, and I intend to spend the rest of my life proving it. The only evidence I have is the happiness I feel when I'm with you, the longing when we're apart."

Her eyes glistened. But then she pulled out of his embrace and gave him a tantalizing smile. "In that case, Detective, we should put off searching the carriage house. Right now, I think a more personal investigation is in order." She took his hand and led him toward their bedroom.

He returned her wicked grin. "I have to warn you, this investigation might go on all night."

"To serve and protect, that's still your motto, right?"

"To love and cherish," he amended. "For the rest of our lives."

"They're asking for you," the clerk announced outside the courtroom doors.

This was the moment Linda had been dreading. As Walter's accountant, she'd known she'd be subpoenaed. Now here she was, less than two weeks later, about to give her statement in a preliminary hearing that would determine whether the case would go to trial.

The D.A. had pressed for a speedy process, and it looked as though he would get his wish. The prosecution was claiming that Walter had been planning an off-shore pickup and that Jeremy had hoped to catch him in the act. Jeremy got what he wanted, but the price had been too high. He'd paid with his life.

The evidence was damning. Backing up the smuggling transactions alluded to in Jeremy's files, the other set of accounting books had been located exactly where Linda had said they'd be, in the attic of the old carriage house.

"Are you all right?" Tyler asked, concern in his voice.

For a moment, an old fear resurfaced. She recalled testifying against Timothy Sands, remembering the threats he'd made against her after he'd been sentenced. She quickly filed the memory away, along with all the other memories she'd once allowed to control her.

She looked up at Tyler, and he gave her hand a gentle squeeze. His eyes told her he was proud of her for her courage. His touch reassured her that his love was unwavering.

She squared her shoulders, and hand in hand they entered the courtroom. After the judge arrived, she was asked to take her place on the witness stand. One hand on the Bible, the other hand raised, she listened solemnly as the clerk swore her in. After she'd pledged to tell the truth, the clerk sat down, and a hush fell over the room.

She caressed the medallion around her neck. "The closest thing to my heart," Tyler had said when he'd given it to her that night at the hotel. It was now the closest thing to *her* heart. No, that's not so, she thought, smiling to herself. Tyler had that distinction. Tyler and their baby.

As if on cue, she felt a stirring inside her. She was only a little more than three months pregnant—too early to feel movement, she'd been told—but nothing could convince her that it wasn't the baby.

"Are you ready to proceed, Mrs. Carlton?" the judge asked.

She looked around the room, then rested her gaze on Tyler. "Yes, I'm ready," she answered with confidence.

It was the whole truth and nothing but the truth. She saw it reflected in her husband's loving eyes.

* * * * *

*Don't miss the emotional conclusion of the
Special Edition continuity*

**THE PARKS EMPIRE
THE HOMECOMING**
by Gina Wilkins

*Coming in December 2004
Available wherever Silhouette Books are sold!*

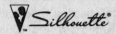

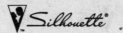

Coming in December from

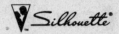

SPECIAL EDITION™

and beloved author

Allison Leigh

THE TRUTH ABOUT THE TYCOON

(SE #1651)

Desperate to see justice served, CEO
Dane Rutherford took matters into his own
hands and headed to Montana to track down
the man who kidnapped his sister. But his
mission got seriously sidetracked when he
literally collided with Hadley Golightly. And it
wasn't long before this tempting brunette was
showing this alpha male that sometimes the
best things in life are the ones you can't control!

Don't miss this captivating new book!

Available at your favorite retail outlet.

Coming December 2004 from

SPECIAL EDITION™

and reader favorite

Sharon De Vita

RIGHTFULLY HIS

SE#1656

Max McCallister had given Sophie the greatest gift—
the children her husband, his brother, hadn't been able
to give her. But not long after Max became sperm donor
and Sophie gave birth, his brother died. After years of
hiding his feelings for the woman he'd always secretly
loved, had the time finally come for Max to claim
what was rightfully his—Sophie and
his twin daughters?

Available at your favorite retail outlet.

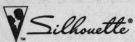

COMING NEXT MONTH